Other Novels by J.L. Walden

Live, Love or Die

Saving Lorelei

The Desolation Valley War

Lethal Difference

Judgement at Molala Ridge

Warlords of Can-Am

Adrian Mikolas

Chakoda's Ghost

Syrian Rescue

The American Coup-Survival

Sci-Fi

Lifeboat to Scorpio

The Winking Planet

300 years in Space

PRESIDENT Who?

A novel by J.L. Walden

<u>Preface</u>

The United States Federal Government is broken. The balance of powers between the House of Representatives, the United States Senate, the Supreme Court, and the Executive branch of the government are not balanced. They no longer represent, or believe in the philosophical foundations of a society the founders of this nation hoped for and tried to initiate.

The behavior of all of the above is controlled by the election cycles and by mankind's insatiable greed for wealth and power. It seems that most people have neither the ability or desire to resist this double-edged ax hacking away at the humanistic hopes for a benevolent and supportive structure of law and equality the founders of the United States of America tried to create.

Many, perhaps most Americans still hope for that dream to be fulfilled; but few really believe it will happen.

Who has the answers?

Where is the leadership?

How do we start back toward the American dream?

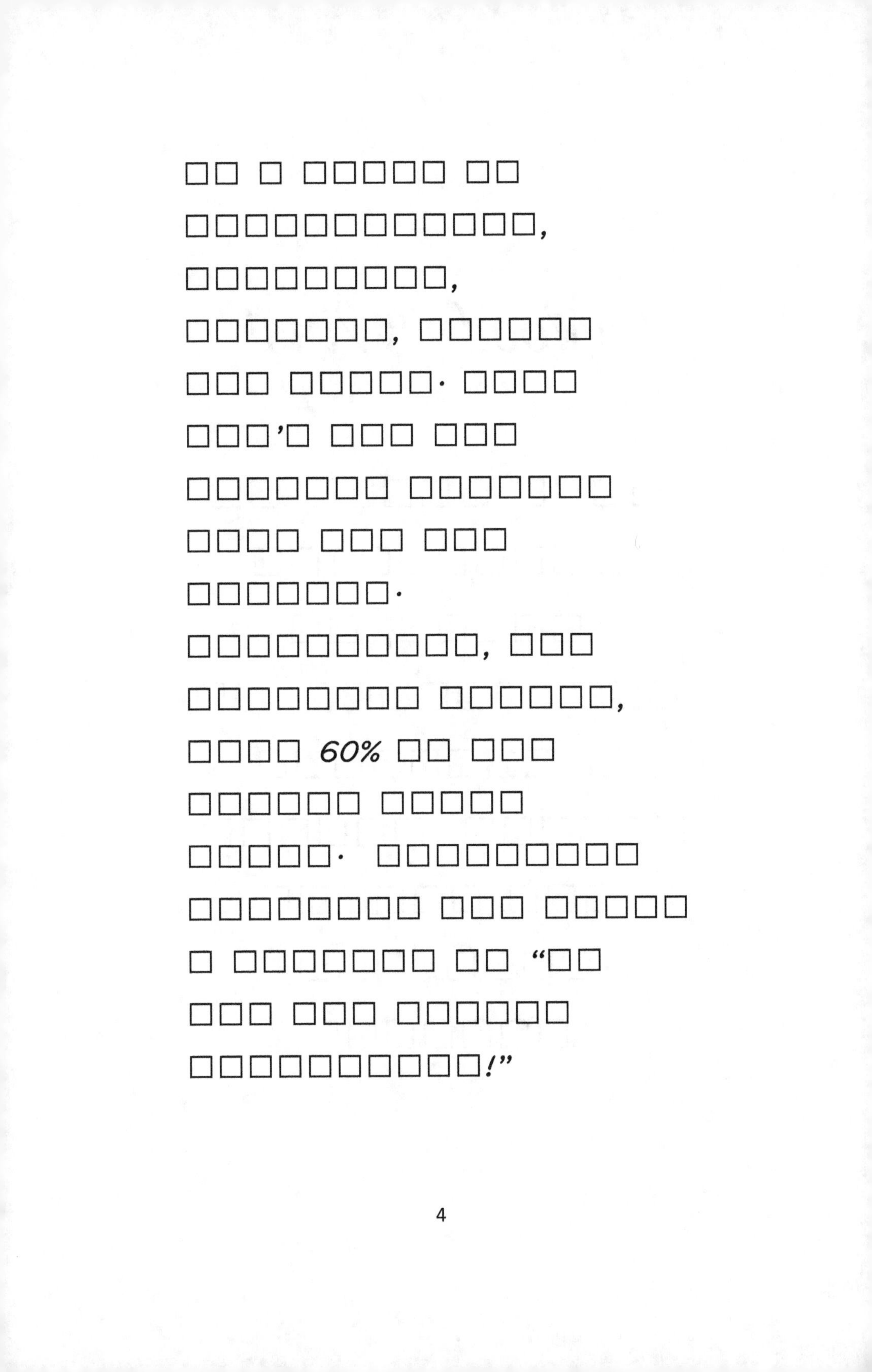

60%

Woody Wins!

□□□□□□□□ □□□□ □□ □□□!

The tall, thin lanky man strides down the hall. The man accompanying him is struggling to keep up; he is somewhat shorter than Heimdall and carries more body fat. Heimdall is six foot four inches tall and used to these fast paces. He was a middle-distance runner on his high school track team, and still runs, for fun, whenever he has the opportunity. He's wearing canvas shoes and sweats.

His Aide is resorting to running a few steps, then walking a few, to keep up. His business suit looks a little rumpled, the coat is unbuttoned, and his tie is swinging back and forth like a clock pendulum.

Bringing up the rear is an older man. He is strolling behind at his own pace. The look on his face states the he 'doesn't give a

damn, he'll get there when he gets there.'
He is in uniform and has four stars on his
shoulders.

Approaching the group from the other
direction is a young woman burdened with
an armload of manila envelopes, all closed
with metal clasps. She gets a little off
balance and drops most of them on the
floor. As she struggles to hold on to the
remaining envelopes she quietly hisses,
"Shit!"

Heimdall slows down, grins and
comes to a stop. He begins to pick up the
dropped envelops and says, "Let me help
you with that. Hold on to what you saved
and I will pick up the 'shit' you just
dropped."

With a smile she replies, "Thank you.
I didn't mean for anyone to hear that."

He smiles back as he says, "My guess
is that 'shit' is part of the common language
around here,"

"I wouldn't know; I'm new here."

"Me, too; my first day."

She smiles and asks, "Oh, which
department."

He smiles, "You wouldn't believe me if
I told you."

She looks him up and down, then says, "From the way you are dressed I would say it would be something physical ... building maintenance, maybe."

After a loud laugh Heimdall says, "You almost got it ... I fix things."

As he put the last envelopes on the stack in her arms he says, "Now, here is a problem; this will never work. The solution requires fewer envelopes, or more woman. Where do these go?"

"Two doors down; on the right."

Heimdall takes two handfuls of envelopes, hands them his aide and says, "Chris, help her out here; take these down to that room and hurry back."

He turns back to the young woman and says, "There, that's done." He nods his head towards the double doors labeled 'Office of the President' and continues; "Now, I have to go in there and start fixing the baggiest pile of 'shit' on this continent."

One of the two Secret Service guards at the doors steps over and opens his half of the entry. President Woodrow Heimdall enters followed by the General.

The guard pauses and waits for the President's aide, who is jogging back down the hall toward the entry.

The young woman stands transfixed, open eyed, and mouth ajar. The envelopes begin to slide off the stack in her arms ... one by one.

In the Executive Meeting Room of the President's Office, seven people, four men and three women, are waiting. They stand up as the President and General enter. The door is held open until the Aide, to the President, Christopher Donavan, arrives, gasping for breath.

He goes through the door, goes to the chairs along the wall, the door closes, and President Heimdall orders. "Please be seated,"

He continues speaking as the group of administrators begin sitting down, "As you all know you will be sworn into office tomorrow, but your work began yesterday as we assumed control of the national government.

"An hour ago, I was sworn in as President and Steven Hightower was sworn in as Vice President.

"A week ago, a Strategic Two Alert was ordered to all military units of the United States Army, Navy Marines, Air Force, and Coast Guard. It is in effect within all states, territories, protectorates, embassies, camps, forts, depots, offices, et cetera.

"Three days ago, all Military Reserve and National Guard units were ordered to stand ready and wait in place.

"Four days ago, we announced to all foreign nations that there was to be an extensive reorganization of our government and that any military action against American properties or people would be considered an 'Act of War.' They could expect immediate and proportional retaliation from our Military to any such actions."

President Heimdall glances back and forth for a moment looking each Cabinet member in the eyes; he then says, "This meeting is to bring you up to date. All the information is in the note books on the table in front of you. Notice that they are labeled, 'For your eyes only.' Believe it, obey it; these note books will not be taken from this room, unless they are in the possession of one or more of the armed guards.

"We will study it here, in this room for the next few hours, or days. The intent of this document is to keep all of you 'in the loop;' it is not a set of orders or guide lines.

"You will be on your own out there, keeping the nation running as the Constitution Committee meets to create and enact a revised Constitution...

"Protection and security of the buildings and grounds of the capital area was developed by and is now commanded by General Douglas Lee Porter; Chairman of the Joint Chiefs of Staff. He is also advising our foreign diplomatic corps for the immediate future.

"I will turn this meeting over to him now.

"I'll be right back, I really need to go relieve my bladder."

There was a wry grin on the General's face as stands up and announces, "He drinks too much coffee; let's take a twenty-minute break. We need our President and his attention with us for our discussions.

Then, in a stern voice he orders, "You heard him about the documents **do not** take your copy of the documents out of this room!"

After the break General Porter returns to the lectern at the head of the long table, President Heimdall sits down on one of chairs along the side wall, his assistant, Christopher Donovan sits down beside him and the others in the room return to their chairs at the table.

General Porter clears his throat and announces, "Come to order; I will begin with a status report of the Military.

"All 'on duty' Military, including Reserves and National Guards are at Strategic Alert Level Three. Where deemed necessary the Alert has been raised to Level Two, which is 'aggressive defense.' Here and there, a few units are at Level One, which is 'aggressive offense.' No further information will be released at this time.

"Reports from our Ambassadors, Consulates, and other representatives overseas are being met with statements of support and cooperation from our allies; silence from almost all others, those less friendly nations.

"One of the first matters we are to consider today is to issue a reminder to those 'less friendly nations' of the scope and power of our nuclear deterrent; *in* our land based silos, our submarines *in* the seas, our fleets *on* the seas, our bombers *in* the skies and our satellites *in orbit.*

"Additionally, there is strong support from our diplomatic corps for a special secret message to be sent to the governments of Russia, China, North Korea, and Iran. It will inform them, 'that now is not a good time to play a game of 'chicken.'

"With all United States troops waiting with fingers on triggers, sailing a paper airplane over a protected area could initiate a global response before anyone could say the word 'negotiate'.   And that concept, 'negotiation' does not exist in our vocabulary at the time being."

General Porter pauses to sip some water and then continues, "The civilian population, all civil servants, education, transportation, information, commercial and industrial operations have been given orders to continue as normal.

"So far there has been about sixty percent compliance, with another twenty percent declaring they are ready to comply, and will, within days. The remaining twenty percent is expected to return to normalcy within a week or so. There has been no interruption of police, emergency services, or hospitals.

"To avoid economic damage all banks and lending services, stock and commodity markets have been ordered closed for one week."

"So, there you have it," General Porter said. "There have been no riots, no demonstrations; not even complaints. It seems that everyone is so sick and tired of the ineffective, disgusting and corrupt circus of the outgoing government that they want to watch and see what happens, what we are going to do.

"The public seems to be saying, 'Here it is, this is your chance, you have promised a lot; so do something, if you can. If you don't, we will give you complaints, demonstrations, riots, and more. We will tear all these white buildings down and set the country on fire."

For a moment General Porter looks around the silent group sitting around the table. He then says, "Mister President, I relinquish the lectern to you."

The President slowly stands up and strolls to the head of the table.   He stands for a moment, apparently deep in thought, then he states, "As the General said, the public has given us a short period of time to show them that things are going to change.   I make it to be a very short time; perhaps a week.   They want to see something happen today. They want to see something in their evening news … … and they will get it.

"In a few hours I will deliver a brief report to the American people of what we have accomplished today.   I will emphasize the formation of the Constitution Committee; and terminating the tenure of each and every Representative and Senator.

"By the way, we confiscated their brief cases, their electronic devices and everything in their desks.

"That should make for some interesting reading."

President Heimdall pauses again, then continues, "I will tell the public that tomorrow morning I will issue a Presidential Order to the Governors of each and every state, and Administrators of each and every territory and domain that they are to operate independently until further notice.

"This order will give the Governors full authority and responsibility for the operation of all departments, offices and whatever else is normally operated by the States. This will include the return of authority over the National Guards to the States. The Military Reserves will remain Federal.

"All classified data is to remain classified, and protected.

"The Federal government will retain all authority and responsibility for operation of federal departments as they currently exist.

"The Pentagon will continue to protect and defend the United States of America and its people in conformity with the established codes and laws."

Heimdall smiles, "Nothing new there; the Military hasn't moved a solder, a vehicle, a gun or coffee pot. There is no military coup, and there is no threat of there being one.

"Almost everyone employed by in the Executive Departments will be sitting at the same desks tomorrow that they are sitting at today. The government will still be up and running tomorrow, as always.

"But there is something else, that will happen tomorrow morning.

"Tomorrow the actions of this administration will bring to the attention of the public, and the bureaucrats, that the existing boundaries and expectations embedded in State and Federal operations are being replaced by a new, different, *effective* set of boundaries and expectations.

"And, the chief executives of departments can accept these changes right now, or they can enjoy their retirement, beginning tomorrow.

They can sit on some park bench, somewhere, feed pigeons and reminisce about 'the good old days' when they had some influence on how things were done, or the authority to shape anything; you know, the good old days when they had a job."

The group sit quietly and Heimdall watches the expressions on their faces. The President turns, walks to the lectern and grips it in hands. He sternly states, "There will be a Constitutional Congress ... there will be a new Declaration of Intent ... there will be new Articles of Operation ... and a New Government will be created and empowered within days!"

President Heimdall briefly pauses and then continues, "The first steps have been taken. The Congress and Senate of the United States and all its' myriad committees, offices of 'this and that;' gaggles of geese honking and squawking about 'who owes what to whom', have all been dismissed and sent back to where they came from.

"Everyone was given one hour to gather their personal items and get out ... no exceptions.

"The lights were turned off, the doors closed and locked, and the premises guarded by the Secret Service, backed up by Federal Marshalls.

"My office has informed me that somewhat over a hundred did not meet the one-hour deadline, they are now confined in various jails around town. They will be processed, and charged with trespass, disorderly conduct and released on their own recognizance, as soon as we can get around to it. It will probably take a day or two.

"Their salaries and expense accounts ended yesterday. They will receive no travel pay to get out of town, they can buy their own damn tickets home.

"Their lifetime, full medical insurance, paid for by the government, will be phased out in about a month.

"Also, there is another practice no rational citizen of this country can understand or tolerate that will soon disappear. Why do members of Congress continue to receive the majority of their salaries and benefits when they retire or resign their position? Even if they serve only one day! And the government even pays for them to operate and staff offices in or near the District of Columbia after their term in office ends. It's absurd! It is costly! It is criminal

"This will change; the Executive Orders are being typed as we meet.

"Hell, this alone might balance the budget.

After a pause for the laughter to die down President Heimdall continues

"A task force is being created to collect and analyze everything left in the offices of former Congress members and their associates. I expect more than a few might end up in prison.

The President pauses for another moment and reads something in his copy of the notebook. He looks up and says, "It seems that our new Justice Department is still in the development stage.

"There will be changes to the Jurisdiction of the Supreme Court, the Superior Court System, and auxiliary portions of the Judiciary system. We want our new government to be based on existing rule of law, relevance, trial procedure, et cetera."

He looks at his Attorney General nominee, Lawrence Nevins, and asks. "Larry, could you get right on this problem of the jailed politicians when we adjourn? We don't want to appear to be punishing people without due process or due cause."

Nevins nods and makes a few quick notes; then looks up at President Heimdall and says, "I'm postponing all active cases to a date 'to be determined.' I am ordering all judges of all federal courts, except the Supreme Court, to immediately switch to processing the disorderedly conduct charges against of those former members of the House of Representatives and Senate; and all their associates that are under arrest. That should break up the log jam."

The President grins, "And float some dead wood downstream, I imagine." President Heimdall glances at his watch and then states, "My, my. How time flies when you are having fun.

"You all know the procedure; please stand."

The seven new Cabinet Officers rose and raised their right hands

The President continues, "You all know and understand the Oath you are about to take; do you accept the responsibility and swear defend the Government of the United States of America faithfully and honestly, to the best of your ability?

There was a chorus of "I do's"

Heimdall smiles and says, "As the President of the United States of America, elected by the citizens of our country, I appoint you as Secretaries of your respective Departments.

Heimdall grins and says, "Now go make things happen. We are meeting here tomorrow; have your reports ready.

"Me and my staff are working the relationships of the divisions of the next government. I can tell you one thing, right now, the concept of 'lobbyist' will soon become so hideous, and so vulgar as to be the grossest of insults.

Lorrain Dumont, Chief of Staff remains in the meeting room after the new cabinet members leave.

Chris Donovan stays in his seat along the wall.

Dumont is a tall and slender woman about six feet. She wears her straight dark brown hair shoulder length, resembling a brown helmet. Her expressive brown eyes do a lot of her talking for her. She is a charmer with her smile and gentle voice; but she scares the hell out of people, when she wants to, with her silent, stern, unblinking stare.

If anyone wants to see the President, they had better have an appointment, a national emergency, or be named Celeste Aileen Mason. Celeste is the President's consort and the mother his two children.

Lorrain and Celeste are good friends and manage the President's appointment calendar smoothly.

Woody walks over to Lorraine, sitting alone and silent in her chair at the table and asks, "How bad is it?"

"Not so bad," she replies. "About what you expected, but it will get noisy. As well as the fifteen who are complying, twenty-two Governors have requested explanations before compliance. Ten Governors refuse to immediately comply, stating they can't, they need more time. Three Governors; South Carolina, Georgia and Alabama challenge the validity of the election and declare independence from any orders from the newly elected President."

The President smiles, "Only three; that's better than we expected. I guess we have more support in Dixieland than we expected."

"Did you say Dixieland or Disneyland?"

The Presidents eyes twinkled as he replied, "Dixieland; if the Disneyland Empire opposed us, we would really be in trouble.

"Let's go to my desk, I have to call General Porter and initiate our response."

Twenty-four hours later all costal ports in South Carolina, Georgia, and Alabama are blockaded by U.S Navy war ships; all international shipping is diverted to other ports. Armed Coast Guard ships are patrolling all major rivers, diverting shipping back to their points of origin and impounding some cargo.

Inland, all interstate and state highway crossings from the three rebellious states to adjacent states are closed by U.S, Army troops. Some cargo is seized or turned back. Treatment of railroad systems is more complex, but similar.

The Pentagon issues orders to all Military personnel in the States surrounding the rebellious states to go to Strac three (armed and in position). Orders are also sent to all National Guard units of the non-complying states to stand down, in place, and wait for further orders. Failure to obey this order will be treated as insurrection. All participants will be immediately arrested and incarcerated in whatever facilities are available. Military Reserve Units receive orders to stand down and take no position.

On day three of the facedown negotiators were sent to the three rebel governors. The message sent was, approximately, *"Really! Are you out of your frigging minds?   The Civil War ended a century and a half ago!"*

The three governors decided to rescind their declaration of independence and joined the group that just wanted more information before complying.

The press referred to it as the 'Four Day Civil Snit Fit.'

The President is on the phone talking to the Secretary of Interior, Roberto Cortez, "Bob, I want the negotiations to originate from your office. I am not a King, Bob, we are a democratically elected administration; elected to run the country; just go out and do it; show the people that we are the *people's government."*

… … …

"Yes, Bob, that's right; the ten Governors requesting more time to comply are those with the highest level of industrialization and social complexity. They have rooms full of complex commitments, agreements and responsibilities which have to be addressed. These ten states; California, New York, Illinois, Texas, Pennsylvania, Massachusetts, Michigan, Ohio, Florida, and Washington, and they are on our side, they just needed some more time.

... ...

"Yes, fifteen Governors are ready to sign without reservation.

"But we need the process completed as soon as possible.

"Which means *you* have to nudge them along as the need arises. You don't need to call me for permission; okay?"

The President hangs up and says to his aide, Chris Donovan, "I guess 'on the job training' is how we are all going to learn how we do what needs doing."

Chris smiles and nods his head.

□□□□□□□ □□□□□

Ramon Diaz-Mondego, Chancellor of University of Florida is working from lap top, he states to the image on the screen, "Without fanfare, hardly noticed, a man comes out of nowhere, runs as an independent; and wins. He is elected President of the United States.

"He campaigned on a platform of returning to the philosophical and social goals of the Declaration of Independence, and the Preamble of the Constitution. He promised his administration would to try again, starting with those documents, and go forward, and create a workable government.

"Now, he wants help! He wants this committee to re-write the Constitution to 'fix the inadequacies' of the original' And he gives us just two weeks to get it done!"

"Take it easy Ramon," **Steven Bradly Jessup**, Chancellor of University of Georgia replies; "It shouldn't be that difficult He insists that we begin with the original Constitution, the Bill of Rights; so that is already done. Then we factor in subsequent amendments as the major guidelines. And then, give consideration to all relevant United States Supreme Court Decisions to bring the Constitution up to date.

"All this is very clear and concise.

"All we have to do is delegate the project to the appropriate professors."

"But, two weeks? For God's sake, we need more time!"

"Think about it Ramon. There are twelve universities on this committee; we divide the task into sections, and each university does one section.

"You know all those professors will have graduate students beating down their doors to be assistants."

"Hmm, I hadn't thought of that; the assistants could even do the research in shifts, around the clock."

The Chancellors are silent as they drift into thought, then Chancellor Diaz-Mondego asks, "Steve, what are you thinking about?"

"Oh," Chancellor Jessup grins. "I was thinking about my name in history books, on the same page as Thomas Jefferson, Alexander Hamilton, Ben Franklin and all the rest of the founding fathers."

"I thought you might be thinking about the books you are going write."

"Yeah, that to; I was also thinking about speaking tours, and television, and maybe a statue or two on law school campuses."

Steve suggested, "Before we get carried away with this celebrity status, don't you think we should go on line and accept the assignment?"

Ramon asks, "Are all our meetings going to be on line?"

"That's right; we will all be linked for fourteen days."

"You know, Steve, my concerns seem to be melting away. How many Chancellors have already committed?"

"Four, you and I should make it six.

"Well then, here's to a better foundation for the Federal Government, a concise and current Constitution, a better nation, and a better person as President. "What's his name?"

"Woodrow Cory Heimdall," Steve replies. He was elected receiving more than sixty per cent of the vote. That was a mandate to proceed with all due haste."

" Yes.; but I do resent the veiled threat in his e-mail; his suggestion that failure to meet the two-week deadline might result in a delay of delivery of all federal grants to our institutions until we come up with a workable plan."

"Well, he did promise the people a new type of government. We had better hope he doesn't get intoxicated with the power the people handed him and become a tyrant."

□□□□□□□ □□□□

Arizona Lieutenant Governor McAlister glances at the two businessmen he is sitting with at the Elks Club in Tucson, Arizona; Henry Masterson, the Sheriff of Santa Cruz County is talking, "I sure wish the Governor could have made it today, I wanted to tell him face to face that I have warned the leaders of that so called 'Posse Comitatus,' that only a Sheriff can organize a Posse, and if they try anything in my county, I would label them a criminal gang and get the State Police and FBI on their asses."

David Ortiz, owner of the local Ford dealership, smiles as he says, "Take it easy

Hank, we all know you can handle those punks, we just wanted to start meeting to discuss how to deal with the new President and these changes he wants.

The anger drains from the Sheriff's face as he says. "Yeah, yeah; I know." He begins gazing across the dining room, looking at nothing in particular.

Ortiz continues, "The biggest issue most of us have is the illegal aliens. What is President Heimdall going do about that? We can't just round them up and shoot them."

"Well, we could," Zeke Conrad, local rancher and current President of the local Cattlemen and Farmers Association chuckles. "Your men could use a little target practice, don't they, Hank?"

Hank shot back, "You're a Nazi, Zeke!"

"Just joking, Hank. But you know how difficult a problem this is. We know we need the cheap labor during planting and harvesting seasons, and more the rest year for menial tasks and services. This has been going on for over a century. It has worked pretty well; the workers come in from Mexico, get there permits to work, the 'green cards', and then, when the work ends they return home. Some, a few, stay and become citizens.

"A few don't return home; their green cards expire and they can't find work. They just hang around, begging, stealing or getting welfare. They are the illegal immigrants; they are the problem.

"And they aren't even Mexican anymore," Kelly Cosgrove, a local realtor, interjects. "For the last few decades thousands of them are coming here from Central America. They have been told they can just walk across the border and automatically become Americans. When they find out it isn't that easy, they find someplace to cross illegally; or, if they have money, they find someone to smuggle them across the border."

Zeke adds, "Most of those stopped at the border don't have the funds or ability to return south; Mexico doesn't know what to do with them either."

Lieutenant Governor McAlister comments, "That is one reason the Governor didn't come to this meeting; there are no answers to this problem yet. The voters up north, in Phoenix, Mesa. Peoria; they don't know how serious this problem is. They hear about it, see it on television news; but they don't live with it.

"The Governor doesn't wish to get involved in this problem until there are some suggestions on how to solve them."

The gloom around the table lasts a few minutes, then McAlister says. "You know, it's really a Federal issue."

"That's right," Ortiz answers. "That's why we are having this meeting. We have to get our message to the new president."

"How; Zeke asks, "We don't have representatives in Washington anymore, Congressmen or Senators. President Heimdall fired them all; kicked them out, sent them home, told them to never come back."

McAllister answers, "I think the President would answer a request from the Governor, requesting information about what to do about illegal immigrants."

Kelly Cosgrove asks, "How are you going to do that, Facebook, Twitter?"

McAllister calmly answers, "Encrypted messages between the Governor's office and the Secretary of the Interiors office."

David Ortiz asks, "Can you get the Governor to do that?"

"I think the Governor wants to do that. He gave me instructions to come back with something. He didn't specify but I believe he wanted a list of your concerns with problems or situations that are best handled on a national level."

The three men look around at each for a moment, then Ortiz states, "We can do that, we can do it right now."

"Good, but you don't need do it right here and now. Make us a list and … … "

The cold, steely stares of the three men stop the Lieutenant Governor's comment in mid-sentence. He begins to worry about the fact that the Sheriff is armed and known for his lack of patience.

"Ah … and maybe you could make an abbreviated list, short statements of the critical issues; and prepare a report with more information, perhaps some suggestions of solutions. That way the Governor could contact President Heimdall's office right away."

"Same old politics; same old bullshit," Zeke growls.

"No, no! The Governor and I are certain that Heimdall's going be a different kind of president; that he will actually get things done. It was congress that always delayed things for months, years. Heimdall got rid of the congress so he could move fast on the most difficult problems."

"Promises, promises. We will make your abbreviated list right now. But we will be watching you, and the Governor, and the President.

Ortiz just happens to have a smart tablet with him. For the next hour the three men work on the 'abbreviated list'.

The Lieutenant Governor reads it through, copies it to his phone, and then sends it to the Governor's encoded phone in Phoenix.

It reads:

Legal Immigration: If a man or woman immigrates to the United States, gets a job and a green card, if after a certain amount of time he becomes an American citizen, then all of his immediate family can apply for citizenship, and have the same rights and benefits as natural born citizens.

In the Latino culture the 'family' is the husband and wife, their children, their parents, brothers and sisters, uncles and, aunts, and cousins. One-person becomes a citizen and his 'tribe' comes across the border to use our public schools, parks, medical facilities and services, and welfare benefits. There is something terribly wrong with this; it has to be fixed.

Illegal Immigration: The southern border of the United States is a joke and it isn't just an Arizona problem; California, New Mexico, and Texas have the same situation. They just walk across the desert or wade across Rio Grande River.

At the core of the problem is those smugglers known as 'Coyotes.' They lie to the peasants in Central America and Mexico and convince them that all they have to do is get to America and they are citizens.

The Coyotes take all the peasant's money, dump them just across the border and leave.

They are criminals, no better than the drug cartels.

Mexico and the United States should get together and declare war on the Coyotes, a hot war. Those who survive should get twenty- to thirty-year sentences.

Second Amendment Rights: Owning and using firearms is part of the American culture. Many Americans don't like that, but their discomfort doesn't give them the right force other Americans to conform to their type of existence.

We are not English; the government can't revoke the Second Amendment and say 'pretty please, give me your guns. More than likely, you will get a bullet or birdshot, instead; traveling at high speed.

When we older men were young it was illegal for common citizens to own automatic firing rifles or ammunition. Only the military and certain police units could have them.

This could easily be enforced, and even supported by gun clubs, if the government just leaves the rest of us alone.

Right to Life: The liberal Americans are never going to agree with Catholics and Fundamental Protestants on the subject of abortion. Nothing is going to change that. The question becomes; does one side have the right to impose their viewpoint on the other side. Nothing is going to change that.

Can the federal Government do anything about it? No; not now.

At the center of the argument is the Constitutional edict of separation of church and state. Court decisions have been too vague and unspecific. Both sides claim the law supports their position.

It should be eliminated and all the Supreme Court decisions with it. Somehow shift the conflict down to the pulpit and the podium, where it belongs. That's where it all started about two centuries ago.

Environmental Protection: We are aware that the Earth's climate change is underway and that as the atmosphere heats up there may be dramatic changes to the lands we live on, the land we farm, and the most precious most commodity of all, water. We, the people, are slowly but surely changing the way we live, the way we work, the way we view our relationship environment.

But, the damage the populations of Earth inflict on the environment is insignificant compared to the damage industry and commerce create and inflict.

As individuals we may be helpless before the greed and arrogance of corporations, but our governments have the power to stop the devastation, or at least, slow it down.

The United States has the largest economy in the world. Surely, we could set an example for the world. If good examples don't work, a little economic pressure might get their attention.

A lot of pressure might actually get a lot done.

Thank you for your consideration, Mister President.

 □□□□□□ □□□□

"Well Celeste, this is your first diplomatic assignment as First Lady, I'm sure you will do very well.   Your presence in your husband's campaign for election always produced positive results."

"Thank you, Mister Secretary, me and my ... *consort* ... and our children have always enjoyed meeting the public.

Secretary of State Charles Morgan seems a little flustered for a moment; he is an older man, in his sixties, quite formal and very traditional. He stammers; "Please forgive my faux pas, I forgot that you and the President are not traditional and did not take vows. I meant no insult Miss, ah, Mistress, ah ...”

With a bright smile she replies, “Let us use given names Charly, it is easier and creates a much friendlier conversation.

Secretary Morgan sighs deeply and says,” Thank you, Celeste; I feel much better now.”

“Good, I took no offense to your refence to ‘vows’, but I would like to give you a little more information on that subject.

“My consort and I took vows, vows to each other. I vowed to be the best woman I can be; he vowed to be the best man he could be; and together we would be the best parents we could be. These vows are the foundation of our family life together.

“They are private; they are personal, and they are sacred to us, above all else.

“We believe in and respect the rights of others to have differing viewpoints and practices, and that patience, tolerance and compromise is necessary for all of us to live together on this planet.

“But, no individual, group of individuals, business organization, religious order, or government agency has the right to impose unnecessary and offensive requirements on others."

Secretary Morgan smiles and comments, "I share your observations and appraisal, but you will have a hard time overseas where religion is often the cornerstone of the government."

"I hope not, We are only visiting some of our closest allies; Great Britain, France, Germany and Italy. And on the way home we will visit Mexico City.

"It's a celebrity visit. It is international public relations. The children and I are to charm the populations and the press.

"But I also have another private mission, which is to explain the operation of the 'interim government' until the 'new government' becomes operational. United States of America Two, will greatly resemble United States of America One; but modernized and streamlined.

"Europeans will recognize the influence of the European democracies that emerged after World War Two. Specifics will not be available for some time but their emergence will be noticed.

"The dissolution of the American Congress was essential before the next government could be formed and installed.

"Right now, America has an autocratic President; perhaps a year from now America will have some form of democratically elected Parliament with a Prime Minister.

"Well, we will see. But that convoluted, self-serving, self-flagellating, incestual debating club we called 'our Congress' has been spanked and sent home."

Charly laughs and adds, "Never to return. But I must suggest that you not use such earthy language in public, Celeste. It is appropriate but not diplomatic."

"Oh, I won't; but they made me sick; and got what they deserved."

"Well, Celeste, we don't have to put up with that riff-raff any more. I have heard that a substantial number of them are on extended vacations overseas; Europe, Asia, Pacific Islands; anywhere but the United States.

"Thanks, Charly."

" You're welcome, Celeste. I am glad to see that you are well informed on the goals of our interim government and what we must accept to get there."

"You shouldn't be surprised, Charly. The man sleeping with me in my bed talks of nothing else."

After an appropriate silence Secretary Morgan clears his throat and then says, "Another matter, Celeste, you must maintain the dignity of your position at all times overseas.

'You must be formal and presidential in diplomatic meetings; anytime you are in the public domain, and even when you are relaxing.

"You and your children will be in the spotlight as you party with the aristocracy *and* the working class. Your charm and beauty and that of your children will be a great asset in winning the respect and cooperation of governments and the populace.

"And one more item, a more sensitive matter, please do not swim in the nude even if others are."

"Oh, for Christ's sake! How am I going to keep my kids out of a pool; they love to swim, in the nude?"

"I don't know Celeste; this is an important matter."

"Charly, anyone, anytime, can go nude on beaches in France and Italy!"

"I don't know what to advise you, Celeste; perhaps just don't go to the beach?"

"Oh, I get it now; I am to be silent and smiling when I am in public; I am to be entertaining, charming and a little flirtatious with important government members, but, for heaven's sake, avoid having any fun with my children.

"I understand, Charly, I do; I am to be the designated 'White House Party Girl.' Thanks a lot. Charly!"

"Celeste ... *Please!*"

"Oh, quit whining, Charly; I'll do it. "But you owe me."

"Agreed, now, there is another matter of great importance. We need to get a top-secret communique from Rome to the White House. "We need your help.

"A one of a kind' designer purse will be presented to you as a gift by the designer when you visit our embassy in Italy. It has been examined and cleared by Italian Security.

"Actually, it contains a top-secret communique encrypted on the product tag of the purse. We need you to carry that purse onto Airforce One; your luggage will not to be scanned at the airport."

"You're kidding."

"I'm not."

"This was definitely not on the job description I was given."

"I'm sorry."

"You sure do say that a lot, Charly. Perhaps you should make a 'I'm Sorry' sticker' and wear it on your breast pocket."

Celeste pauses and is thoughtful for a moment. She then says, "Let me see; I'm the President's, wife, the mother of his children. I must act dignified and be diplomatic at gatherings, but up close up I must be charming, a little flirty, perhaps a little sexy, like all 'party girls' do. In my spare time I am a spy and a smuggler.

"What's next, Charly? Is the British, spy 007, going to drop out of a helicopter and rescue me from the bad guys? Is he going to carry me away to safety; save my life?

"If so, Charly, I want Sean Connery; he was the first actor to play 007, and the best looking."

Secretary Morgan waits silently during Celeste's oration.

Finally, Celeste states, "Alright; I'll do it; but I'm serious about Sean Connery.

"Celeste, he a rather elderly man now."

With a withering glance she answers, "So?"

□□□□□□□ □□□

A meeting of the Economic Counsel of the Parliament of the British Commonwealth is in progress.

Prime Minister, Carlyle Hastings, is shouting about the startling events in the United States of America.

"Who is this Woodrow Heimdall; what is his background, does he have any experience in governing, business, or commerce, or ... or ... was he ever in the military?"

One council member answers, "We know nothing about him, Sir; no one paid any attention to him when he filed as a candidate for President, he was the least likely to be elected. He campaigned on a promise to re-write the American Constitution ... the Constitution, for heaven's sake!"

Another member interjects, "We know he is married, and has two young children. We know he is wealthy, quite wealthy; he funded his own campaign. I believe it was from investments, stock market, bonds, and whatever."

The Prime Minister wipes his forehead with his handkerchief and quietly asks, "Has the Yard, or M-16 investigated his past?"

"I'm sure they have, Sir, but we don't have copies."

As the Prime Minister's face reddens, he begins to perspire again, "And has anyone thought to *ask* any of our Security Departments for a report on the man who just became the leader of the most powerful nation on earth!?"

"Sir, we are just the Economic Council, we don't have the authority to ask for ..."

"Well, I do!" the Prime Minister roars!"

He turns to his Aide sitting in one the chairs along the wall and quietly asks, "Mister Darby, would you please go and request what I need. Stick with it until you get high enough in the chicken yard pecking order that you are talking with someone who will do something."

Mister Darby grins and says, "Aye Sir, I will get done, Sir."

He closes his laptop, stands up and hustles out the door.

The room is silent as everyone waits for the next words from the Prime Minister. It is a minute or so before he regains his composure. His voice is steady and firm as he says, "Whoever he is, whatever he does, it will have a negative effect on the markets., all of them, everywhere. Investors do not like uncertainty. And that will rather quickly depress our markets.

"As one of their largest trading partners we must hope for a short negative cycle and a quick rebound.

"We must support our currency during the downturn to stay out of a national recession.

"We must see that there is enough liquidity in our reserves to move rapidly.

"We must be ready to absorb a piece of this economic chaos that will be caused by the election of this unknown financier and politician, Mister Heimdall."

The Prime Minister pauses for a moment, takes a sip of water and then continues, "I am advising you to formulate our economic plans without the usual haggling, arguing and political posturing; time is of the essence.

"My Office will contact our international trading partners and initiate conversations about coordinated our economic plans.

"I really must get back to my Office and proceed with my tasks; I'm sure you will continue with this urgent situation."

After the Prime Minister leaves a buzz of conversations fills the room.

Back in his office Prime Minister Hastings notices a slip of paper on his desk. He recognizes it as his personal secretaries handwriting. On it is a man's name, 'Jonathan Haywood,' and a few words. 'Important information, for your eyes only, urgent, he will wait.'

He switches on the speaker phone and asks, "Agnes, who is this Jonathan Haywood and is he still here?"

"Sir; he is still here, waiting, and will not offer any further information to anyone but you. He is casually dressed with a loose, waist length jacket, no hat, no packages or satchels."

"Does he look dangerous to you?"

"No, he looks terrified, to me. William has signaled me that he sees no danger."

"Hmm, well let's hope you are both correct; have William escort him in."

A few moments later the door to the waiting room opens, William, a six foot two, well-muscled former Rugby star is practically dragging the much smaller and thinner Jonatan Haywood into the room. They cross over to the chair in front of the Prime Ministers desk. William gives him a full body pat down including crotch and buttocks and then sits him down in the visitor's chair."

For a moment the Prime Minister stares at the visitor who is visibly trembling, he then says, "Well, Mister Heywood, now that you have experienced your government in action, perhaps you will tell me who sent you, and what is the information you have for me."

"Yes Sir, I ... ah ... I was told you would understand."

Carlyle Hastings stares at him for a moment and then says, "Perhaps; continue."

"He ... he said I was to give you a code word, and you would understand. He said he was afraid I would forget it, so he wrote it on my forearm.

As Jonathan Haywood reaches into his coat to take it off, one of Williams massive hands slams down on Haywood's shoulder and an automatic pistol magically appears in the body guards other hand.

William speaks for the first time, his deep baritone is just barely above a whisper, "Take off your coat, slowly, and show us your forearm."

Haywood complies; the message is 'ORB 5 up 7 next.'

William and Hastings stare at each other for a moment, and then the Prime Minister says, "Mister Haywood, I recognize the meaning of this code word and it is top secret. I am sorry to inform you that you will be our guest for a day or two, until the meaning of this code is no longer secret."

"But ... but ..."

"There are no alternatives, Mister Haywood. You will be in a luxury apartment, with television and all the movie channels and on line games. You will be provided with food and drink of your choice.

"Is there anyone who will wonder where you are."

"Uh ...No, no one."

"Good, good, if you need anything, or there someone you want to call, just ask the guards at your room."

"Guards?"

"Don't worry, we will take care of everything for a few days."

Two guards, both looking similar to William arrive and take Jonathan away.

After they are gone the Prime Minister looks at William and asks, "Do you know what ORB 5 ready 7 means?"

"More or less, Sir. Not the details. Sir. I know of ORB; I know of the ten levels; seven is pretty high."

The Prime Minister, still sitting at his desk, leans forward and puts his elbows on the desktop.

He then lowers his forehead into his open palms. He mummers out loud, "I tried to reach out to that wild eyed American. I tried to get his attention before he did something really stupid. I tried ... I did ... there just wasn't enough time."

William calmly comments, "If he pulls it off, Sir, it will be a turning point in history. He may be as famous as Winston Churchill."

The Prime Minister replies, "Or Adolf Hitler."

□□□□□□□ □□□□□

Attorney General Lawrence Nevins is in the Oval Office with President Heimdall. They both have copies of a document under discussion.

Secretary of State, Charles Morgan, and Secretary of Interior, Roberto Cortez, are also at the meeting.

The President says, "Larry, I know this Order is a major change, and there will moaning, groaning and howling throughout the nation; but it has to be done, and you have to implement it.

"Illegal immigration is a crime and will not be tolerated, we will see to that after we fix the '*legal*'immigration problem.

"Currently, if a man or woman immigrates to the United States, gets a job and a green card, and lives in the United States for a certain amount of time, he or she may apply to become an American citizen.

"The FBI and NSA then investigate their personal history and background and give or withhold residency approval. They may eventually apply for citizenship and live in America during the application procedure, which takes years.

"When he or she can read simple English, and pass a written test on the history and culture of America, he or she is then entitled to receive citizenship.

"This procedure takes several years. During this time the applicant and all of their immediate family are entitled to live in the United States and receive all the benefits and privileges of natural born citizens; cetera.

"Once this person is a citizen all of his immediate family can apply for citizenship, and have the same rights and benefits as natural born citizens. In the Latino culture the 'family' is the husband and wife, their children, their parents, brothers and sisters, uncles and, aunts, and all their cousins.

"And, any child of any one in this family, born in the United States is automatically a citizen.

"One person becomes a citizen and his whole 'tribe' comes across the border to use our public schools, parks, medical facilities and services, and welfare benefits. *There is something terribly wrong with this!* This is intolerable; it has to be changed!"

The Attorney General sits quietly and waits.

"And it will be;" the President states. "You have before you a copy of the Presidential Order changing and clarifying the definition of 'immediate family.' Henceforth, in the United States, we will use *our* countries definition of 'immediate family.' The family is birth mother and father and their natural born children only.

Alternate procedures and special consideration will be given to step mothers and fathers, and adopted children. Dependent grandparents may also be considered; we have no intention of breaking up families, but 'last minute additions' will not be accepted.

"We are also revising the 'children born of foreign citizens in the United States.

At least one parent must be an American citizen residing in the United States for twenty-four consecutive months."

He pauses for a moment and then continues, "We are aware of the problems in the rest of the world, and have sympathy for the poverty, hunger and misery of their disenfranchised populations. But we cannot solve their problems in their countries by importing the very causes of their failures, to our country.

"Yet, that is what we have been doing.

"We will not continue to be the dumping ground for other countries failures.

He pauses again and then announces, "We are currently studying another change. Our friend and neighbor to the north, Canada, approaches immigration from a different perspective.

'Once a year their Administration reviews their national census. They also annualize the projected manpower needs for all segments of their economy; doctors, other medical specialists, pharmacists, bank clerks, farmers, auto mechanics, school teachers, stage entertainers, cooks, cleaners ... even manicurists and lawyers.

"Wait a minute ... I need to check that 'lawyers' number.

"Well; my, my.

"The fact is, these numbers are ranked in importance to their economy and immigration is granted on the basis of manpower needs; not on who one is related to, or what language they speak, what religion they practice, what country come from, race, creed, sexual orientation, or which damned ball club they are going to play for.

"A single, simple question is asked, "We have this job, in this place, paying this amount of money; do you want to immigrate to this place and do this job? If you do, would you like to become a citizen? It isn't mandatory; the applicant may opt for a temporary green card."

"We may not want to, or be able to just copy the Canadian Model, but it sure spotlights what can be done.

"Questions? Comments?"
Attorney General Nevins scratches his chin whiskers for a moment then states," I don't know how we go about doing this within the current laws, Woody."

"Larry, there are no current laws!."

"I ... I ... Woody where do I start?"

"Hmm; let's see, ah ... I think the best bet is to start with the Canadian Model; when you find something that won't work well for us, you go back to the U.S. rule book and find something that seems to make sense, like keeping step children with the primary family.

"Get something together that I can give to the Constitutional Committee. Whatever it is you cobble together, get it to me tomorrow morning; I will submit it that committee tomorrow afternoon."

"For Christ's sake, Woody; tomorrow morning? Whatever I have will be a mess."

The President gazes at the wall for a moment; then he calmly states, "You are right, Larry, whatever you have tomorrow will be a mess."

After pausing for a moment, the President then states, "Larry, after lunch there is the meeting of all Cabinets leaders. I called you in early because, as Attorney General, you are my confidant and legal advisor. You will be in the driver's seat as go into the greatest change in our government since the Civil War.

"I need you to be my monitor, my advisor, the one who does not fear my office, and the one who holds up the red flag and yells '*Stop; go no further, step back!*"

"Charley, Roberto; you are here because the new regulations will overlap into State and Interior. We will need your input as we get into this.

"Are you willing to accept that responsibility?"

After a moment's thought Attorney Genera Nevins states, "It will be an honor, Mister President. I hope I can live up to your expectations."

"The other two Secretaries quickly agreed.

At two o'clock in the afternoon all cabinet Secretaries plus the Chief of Staff and a Rear Admiral representing the Pentagon sit in the meeting room, waiting for President Heimdall to explain what more he is expecting from them.

He gazes around the room and looks at each person. His voice has a strange, icy tone as he says, "Tomorrow morning each and every one of you will hand me the mess that you created while trying to fix the mess that exists in your departments.

"Right now, all any of you are capable of doing, is creating a mess out of a preexisting mess. That is because you are all trying to be the reincarnations of the demons that created the mess we inherited. You are trying to tinker with that chaos but afraid to use your unadulterated genius to parent something new.

"I had hoped you would immediately comprehend the significance of what is happening here and now. I had hoped for immediate enlightenment and dedication from you who are here.

"It embarrasses me to talk to you like this. I hope it embarrasses you to *be* talked to like this. I hope that when you walk out this room, you all realize that continuing down the road we have all known, is the road back into Hell.

"The world we and our children have to cope with today and in the near future has chemicals and plastic polluted seas, lakes and water ways.

"The air is so polluted that it cannot be breathed in large cities.

"The ozone layer that used to be over the Arctic and Antarctic poles no longer protects us from the ultraviolet rays from the sun.

"As the temperature of the atmosphere rises so does the sea level. We have about half a century to stop the heating of the sea and the atmosphere. If we don't most of the world's harbors will be under water. Intercontinental trade will cease; without that trade civilization will crumble and the human race will become extinct.

"One definition of insanity is to keep repeating same behavior and expecting different results. Failure is guaranteed. Failure is no longer acceptable.

There was a long silence. Then the President says, "Ladies, gentlemen; tomorrow morning; ten in the morning; your report on your particular mess; on my desk; don't be late. And prepare for a long day.

"Retraining our minds to think differently, to clear our brains of archaic assumptions and useless data, to create planning and methods of implementation, will be neither quick nor easy; but we must begin.

"This room will be our school and workshop; we will meet each morning at ten o'clock; break for lunch and deal with emergencies in our Departments and reassemble and one o'clock to continue our discussions. Well will talk, discuss, agree, disagree, get angry, argue, leave the room to pace the halls, return and try again.

"We will get a consensus and create a government that works.

"I am confident that we will have something better than what we had before. It may not be perfect, but it will much better than any of our preceding government, and, maybe, we are setting the precedent for our government to renovate, ventilate and percolate itself every few decades.

"So, let us break for now, get back to our Departments and organize then for our schedule; and return at two."

As the Department Secretaries get up and file out the door, Chief of Staff: Lorrain Dumont has her napkin up to her face. She is hiding her muffled chuckles. As the last official goes through the door she breaks out into loud guffaws.

She slaps her hand on the table, hard, as she laughs. Her laughs become chuckles as she looks at her hand and frowns. She touches her reddened hand and says, "Ow! Damned hard table."

She smiles as she continues out loud, "Love that man. Power; he loves it, he uses it, he never looks back. Nothing is going to stop him."

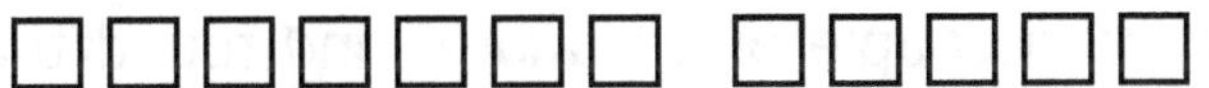

Heimdall is casually speaking to the Cabinet members, everyone had arrived early. Some are sitting, some are standing, most had a cup of coffee. Attorney General Lawrence Nevins states, I don't know how you did it, Woody; two months."

"Oh, it just took a little creative managing, a little push here, a little shove there, an occasional comment that I was considering them as Ambassador to Bangladesh, Mongolia or Zambia. They found ways to get things done.

"Two months after the inauguration and we have a busy Constitution Committee with a first draft of a new Constitution and Bill of Rights, a Reorganized Court System and the framework of the new congress.

"Sure, it is ragged around the edges, with gaps and less than desired overlaps, but that will be corrected over time."

Secretary of Interior, Roberto Cortez asks, "How did you manage the safety and privacy of the Committees 'proceedings?"

"Well, Bob, I turned it over to the Secret Service. I checked on how they were doing a couple of days later and found that no vehicular traffic is allowed within two blocks of the protected locations, except for military vehicles, that is.

"All foot traffic is subjected a through personal screening and search procedure, similar to those at International Airports in the United States.

"All entry points to protected areas are guarded by multiple U.S. Army soldiers with assault rifles. Approximately forty yards within the property lines a series of mobile watch towers are in place, each armed with machine guns.

"Armed jeeps patrol inside the perimeters. Armed Predator drones are overhead.

"No press personal or equipment are allowed within the forty-yard perimeter or at its entry gates.

"Any and all violators would be subject to immediate arrest and incarceration for as long as the Committee is in session."

There was short silence in the room; then the President states, "Relax, it is temporary, we have not become a police state. I wanted to send a loud and clear message to the media that the wild west shouting matches they called 'press conferences' has come to an end. From here on they will sit down, shut up, and raise their hands to be recognized.

"Shall we sit down and begin?"

The President chuckles as he says, "That sounds like a good idea."

When everyone is seated the President begins, "You all have official copies of the report before you; I'm just going to breeze through the major points; ask questions whenever and wherever; ... but ... please raise your hand."

He looks around and then continues,

"We will not have elected officials until we can have a national election, but we will tumble forward by Executive Orders for a while. We will proceed with the results of the recent election as our guideline.

"First and foremost, the Constitution Committee has suggested that the "Electoral College" be eliminated and never be mentioned again. The President and Vice President will be elected by a simple majority of the registered voters of the citizens of the United States, and its Protectorates. It is suggested that the President and Vice President run as a team, just as they currently do.

"Now the big one; the current the Senate will be replaced by a new division of representation and responsibility, which will be the Senate of American Republics.

"And the House of Representatives will be replaced by a Citizens Parliament."

Attorney General Nevins hand flips up as he asks, "Like England?"

"Sort of, Larry, but more like Canada. The British Parliament is burdened with complex relationships with the Royalty and the House of Lords which is hereditary, not elected. We will have none of that in America.

"What is being suggested for our new government is three separate levels of governance, each level dealing with those matters most relevant to their census area.

"This is modeled on our court system; but different, of course. Our Supreme Court adjudicates matters affecting the nation; the Superior Court system operates on a state level; and Municipal Courts operate on county and city level.

"So, we will have four levels of Government: National, Republics, States, and various levels of Municipal.

Althea Johnson, Secretary of Treasury raises her hand and asks, "Woody, we don't have Republics, we have States. I read ahead a little way and it suggests that 'Republics are a group of States, and States are groups of Districts. Where does all of this come from?"

"Good question, Althea. We have to create them; and it won't be easy. What the report called 'Districts used to be called counties. And counties are a group of precincts."

"Easy," Althea interjects, "We are going to need our Army, Navy ... and our Air Force to make that kind of change!"

"Understood, Althea; let's include the Coast Guard, too. We are looking forward at probable resistance, especially at the precinct level.

"Let me remind you, every ten years there is a national census of the population; and the boundaries' of the precincts are re-drawn by the governments of the States in which they are located.

This practice causes and supports gerrymandering, the grouping together precincts in a manner which benefits one group at the expense of another.

Political parties, representing only the rich and powerful individuals and companies, have had a banquet in many States for too long, while working class starves on table scraps.

"Althea, that will now be absolutely unacceptable. We are going to make it impossible for the rich and powerful to have the ability to Gerrymander the precincts. They will no longer able to have one neighborhood with one vote representing twenty of the rich; and another across town with one vote representing five thousand of the poor.

The States will no longer have total power to create the boundaries of precincts; a Federal Bureau of Census will be created to monitor and police the States handling of precincts.

"Oh shit," Althea Johnson mumbled as she fingered the edge of her copy of the report.

The President pauses for a moment and then continues, "Althea, you were a ball of 'cleansing fire' before we were elected. This is your opportunity re-ignite that fire; the National Census Bureau, is part of the Treasury Department."

After a deep sigh Secretary Johnson said, "I hear you, Mister President; and I thank you. I lost sight of our end game there for a moment. But I'm going to need a lot more man and woman power to unscramble those precincts."

"You'll have it. One of my major goals is to kill the Gerrymander beast and bury it so deep that the fires of hell will feast on it."

The President pauses for a moment, takes a drink of water and then says, "Just before this meeting I was informed by the Republic Formation Committee that they have a first draft of the geographic boundaries and names of the proposed Republics. It is still a work in progress and this may change. I have ordered copies sent to your electronics, but I will read the list I have."

"The Commonwealth of Eight American Republics.
North Pacific: "Evergreen Republic"
Three states: Washington, Oregon, Alaska.
Republic of California: "Golden State Republic"
Six states: Golden Gate, Sylvania, Central California, Big Valley, Mojave/Sierra, South California.
Great Plains Republic: "Big Sky Republic"
Nine states: Colorado, Utah, Idaho, Montana, North Dakota, South Dakota, Kansas, Nebraska and Iowa.
Southwest Republic: "Wild West"
Five States: Texas, Oklahoma, New Mexico, Arizona, and Nevada.
Great Lakes Republic: "Heartland"
Eight States: Minnesota, Wisconsin, Michigan, Illinois, Indiana, Ohio, Indiana, Kentucky and West Virginia.
New England Republic: "Patriots"

Six States: Maine, New Hampshire, Vermont, Massachusetts, Connecticut, and Rhodes Island.
Old Dominion Republic: "First Communes"
Seven States: Virginia, Maryland, Delaware, New York, Gotham (formerly NYC), New Jersey and Pennsylvania.
Southeastern Republic: "Dixie"
Eight States: Arkansas, Tennessee, Louisiana, Mississippi, Alabama, Georgia, North Carolina, South Carolina. (The Florida Panhandle and north central Florida is in the process of being annexed to Alabama and Georgia.

There will be three **Territories and Protectorates**
The District of Columbia
The Gulf Protectorate: Puerto Rico, South Florida, various other islands.
The Pacific Protectorate: Hawaii, Guam and other Pacific Islands."

The President pauses and then says, "That's it; that is the Commonwealth of American Republics."

Secretary Cortez asks, "Why did they chop up Florida? When did New York City become a State?"

"Yesterday, maybe this morning, Bob."

"Why?"

"Ask the committee, Bob. Put it in writing, send an e-mail. They are still in session trying to figure out the details of the powers and authority of the Republics."

"And also, how to pay for all of this, I hope."

"That's right, Bob."

Chris Donovan, Heimdall's clerk, comes bustling through the door, goes straight to the President and hands him a note.

After a quick glance at the note Heimdall announces, "I'm sorry, this is a matter requiring immediate attention, we will adjourn until tomorrow, same time.

"Morgan, Sullivan; I need a few moments."

The Secretaries of State and Defense sit back down.

Lorrain Dumont ushers the other Cabinet members out and shuts the door.

The President begins, "As you know, the Government of Iran is blaming the United States for the disappearance of one of their ships. They are raising Hell and vowing to get revenge, to answer in kind.

"It's absurd, our fleet in the Arabian Sea hasn't fired a shot, isn't even on alert."

"That note was from General Porter, he is in the Pentagon War right now. He informs me that what looks like the entire Iranian navy is on alert and moving. Two cruisers, two destroyers and accompanying gunboats are moving towards the Arabian Sea.

"General Porter is tired of their bull shit; I'm tired of their bull shit; the American people are tired of their bullshit!

"Unless you can come up with a good reason not to, I'm going to order the carrier, Gerald Ford, and our Arabian Sea Cruiser Fleet to "Battle Ready."

After a short moment of silence Secretary of State, Charles Morgan askes, "What about Iran's allies?"

"Who knows what they will do other than make a lot of noise?"

"Are you leaving open paths for negotiation?"

"Not as yet, I need you to do that, Morgan.

"I will need some time.'"

"How much will you need?"

"As much as you can give me. Remember, it is approaching noon here; It is approaching midnight in most of Europe."

"Okay. When our fleet begins to move the world will notice. Within one hour all major military powers will wonder what we are doing.

"We will maintain radio silence and answer no questions. By hour two the Iranian government should be in a state of panic; this is what we hope for."

"That gives you two hours to notify our allies that we have no intentions beyond stopping the harassment of our ships in the Arabian Sea. But, we are 'Battle Ready' and we will return fire if interfered with. Can you do that?"

"Oh, yes. I will contact England, France, Italy and Japan first and ask that they relay the message to all their allies. That should do it."

"What about Russia and China the President asks?"

"No need, their espionage systems usually pass information as fast as our diplomatic channels do; they will probably call you."

The President chuckles; "You think? And, like a rude boy after a bad first date? I won't answer."

The Secretary of State grins and comments, "Well It might be a good time for a little ass kicking.   Just enough to embarrass which ever country or countries want to test our resolve."

Woody chuckles, "Really Charly; and I thought you were a gentleman."

"Woody, like all successful politicians in this world, beneath my persona of dignity, honesty and openness there is a fully developed scoundrel seeking influence, power, and control in order to put things the 'right way;' as I see them.

"Fortunately, a lot of us have good intentions, most of the time."

Woody laughs, "Two hours, Charly, two hours."

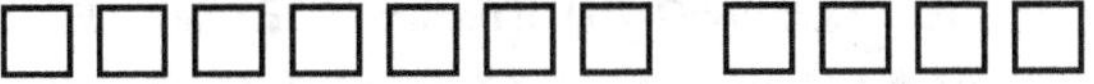

Prime Minister, Carlyle Hastings looks at the man who appears to be a civilian in a conservative business suit but is actually Sir Clinton Baker, Minister of Britain's Intelligence Service, commonly known to M-16. The Prime Minister asks, "Well, Clinton, do you have anything for me?"

"We do Carl. The investigation of the American President and his wife is still in progress but we have enough to put together good profiles of their personalities, their preferences, their weaknesses, what motivates them and what they avoid.

"Woody Heimdall is a forty-five-year-old male American citizen, born in Pennsylvania, he went to grade school in

Philadelphia, Pennsylvania, where his parents were born and raised.

"His parents moved to suburban Chicago, Illinois where he went through middle school, grades seven and eight. His parent's family later moved to Denver, Colorado where he completed High School, grades nine through twelve

He received an intellectual scholarship and started college at Stanford University in California. He spent two years at Stanford, then dropped out and took a job in San Jose's Silicon Valley. He worked, part time, and went to San Jose State University, part time, receiving a Bachelor's degree in Economics.

"He worked as a market analyst for a major brokerage firm for a few years his specialty was macro-economic trends. He was very, very good at spotting startups and established companies that were ahead of demand trends.

At the age of twenty-six he began his own investing. Four years later, at the age of thirty-two, his net worth was ten million dollars.

"He started with a moderate investment in Microsoft and rode out the ups and downs of the company stock for several years.

"Then he began to diversify. One of his investments was Amazon, which he still holds; others are Walmart, General Foods and several large companies specializing in military weaponry and aircraft. His investment strategy appears to be 'buy and hold, reinvesting about ninety percent of his capital gains.'

" He is currently a multi-billionaire at age forty-five. Financing his campaign for President didn't seem to slow down his wealth appreciation at all.

"Our research has revealed that Heimdall's attorneys are in the process of transferring all his investment assets to a blind trust, which he promised to do in his campaign for election.

"At the age of forty he announced that he was thinking about running for President of the United States as an independent.

"He stated that he believed that the President, he or she, must not represent just a political party; he or she must represent the entire population. Anything else has proven to be divisive, difficult to implement and in violation of the values, ethics and desires of the people of the United States of America.

"The President and his consort are not married; neither the president nor his consort, Celeste Aileen Mason, have ever been married to anyone. However, he and his female partner have a committed relationship. It was just verbal until they had two children, they then decided to have a formal document. The document has never been made public. Whatever that agreement contains, we probably will never know.

"To paraphrase Miss Mason's answer to the question, "It is none of our damn business."

"The answer from Woodrow Heimdall was equally non-comital, consisting of the words, "Whatever she said."

"They have two children; a boy, nine, and a girl, seven. The Presidential couple say they are thinking about having a couple more, but will probably adopt.

"Appearances are that this is a happy, traditional, upper middle-class family with an incredibly stable income and traditional white American values and life styles.

"Most people who were polled about their lack of a traditional marriage vows expressed a cavalier attitude of, "Who cares about that? Someone has to fix this government!"

"We experienced similar attitudes when we asked about their racially mixed ancestry. He is one quarter Native American, Eastern Iroquois, with the remaining three quarters a mixture of various European peoples (primarily German, Swedish and Scotch).

"She is mostly a decedent of European stock; French, English and Spanish, with some undetermined amount of African American DNA.

"American English is their base language, but both are fluent in Spanish. She is also conversant in French and Cajun; she was born in Baton Rouge, Louisiana.

"He is six foot, four inches tall, two hundred and twenty pounds, straight black hair and eye brows, hazel color eyes with a slight epicanthic fold, high cheek bones, and very light tan skin color. He has an athletic build; he still works out some, runs a little more than some, and believes that with physical fitness and a reasonable diet he can live an active life for a hundred years.

"She is five foot ten, one hundred and fifty pounds, medium brown, slightly curly hair and light blue eyes. She has a trim and heathy looking body; her face is well proportioned and has a 'pretty girl next door' good looks and demeanor.

"A common remark about her was, "Rooms brighten up and men feel years younger when she arrives.

"She works out as much as her husband. She tends to swim a lot; in the nude. Her children often join her. So does her husband, every once in a while. They have a pool about half the size of an Olympic Pool in their back yard in Santa Clara County, California. That county is better known as 'Silicone Valley.

"His home is on a twenty-acre site. There is a twelve-foot-high, chain link and Italian Cypress fence around the pool and veranda.

"The top of the fence is electrified, and the pool is only visible from inside the home, the veranda and the back yard.

"About four blocks away he has a three-story apartment building which houses some of his residence staff including the armed guards who monitor the security camera system of the home site.

"The lower floor contains offices, retail shops, a restaurant, some recreation facilities, and a pre-school. There is resident parking in the basement.

"His fortress," the Prime Minister comments.

"Indeed," Sir Baker replies. "He owns a great deal of the real estate within a couple of miles of his fortress.

"She has a Bachelor's Degree in Political Science. She reads about one non-fiction book a week on diverse subjects. She seldom reads novels, and once commented, "Why should I read romantic novels? I'm living one; and I love it!"

"They met at an economic conference in New Orleans. Two weeks later they were living together in a committed relationship.

"They both are on record as considering marriage as practiced in the developed world, an imposition forced on the people by religions and governments. They consider it to be insulting, degrading, manipulative and harmful to everyone;

except the highest authorities of those religions and governments.

"She loves crowds and they love her. She has a great sense of humor but little tolerance for hypocrisy, racism, snide gossip, lying, greed, and more this and that.

"Her ability to shred and disperse the ego, confidence and arrogance of those who challenge her viewpoints on those subjects, is legendary.

"That is all we have, Sir."

"Thank you, Clinton. We will get to meet her and her children fairly soon, she will be in London as a part of a diplomatic tour in a few weeks.

"A college degree in Political Science, you say. I wonder if she will have any political goals with this visit."

"She was active during her mate's election campaign, and along with her glamor she created a great deal of energy and commitment when she spoke to audiences."

"Hmm; this should be interesting."

□□□□□□□ □□□

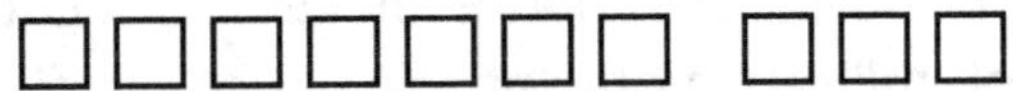

Heimdall is casually speaking to the Cabinet members, everyone arrived early. Some are sitting, some are standing, most had a cup of coffee. Attorney General Lawrence Nevins states, I don't know how you did it, Woody; five days. "

"Oh, it just took a little creative managing, a little push here, a little shove there, an occasional suggestion that they would make excellent ambassador to Bangladesh, Zambia or Mongolia, but they did it. Five days after the inauguration and we have the organization of the new government. Sure, it is ragged around the edges, with gaps and less than desired overlaps, but that will be corrected over time."

"How did you deal with their safety and prevent interruptions?" Secretary of Interior, Roberto Cortez asks.

"Well, Bob, I turned the protection and privacy of the Committee meeting over to the Secret Service. I checked on how they were doing a couple of hours later and found that no vehicular traffic was allowed within two blocks of the protected locations, except military vehicles. All foot traffic was subjected a through personal screening and search procedure, similar to those at International Airports in the United States.

"All entry points to protected areas were guarded by multiple U.S. Army soldiers with assault rifles. Approximately forty yards within the property lines a series of mobile watch towers were in place, each armed with machine guns.

"Armed jeeps patrolled inside the perimeters. Armed Predator drones were overhead.

"No press personal or equipment were allowed within the forty-yard perimeter or at its entry gates. And any and all violators would be subject to immediate arrest and incarceration for as long as the Committee is in session.

"There was short silence in the room; then the President stated, "Relax, it is temporary, we have not become a police state. I wanted to send a loud and clear message to the media that the wild west shouting matches they call 'press conferences' has come to an end. They will sit down, shut up, and raise their hands to be recognized.

"Shall we sit down and begin?"

The President chuckled and replies, "That might be a good Idea, Bob"

When everyone was seated President began, "You all have official copies of the report before you; I'm just going to breeze through the major points; ask questions whenever and wherever; ... but ... please raise your hand."

He looked around and then continued,

"We will not have elected officials until we can have a national election, but we will tumble forward by Executive Orders for a while. We will proceed with the results of the recent election as our guideline.

"First and foremost, the Constitution Committee has suggested that the "Electoral College" be eliminated and never be mentioned again. The President and Vice President will be elected a simple majority of the registered voters of the citizens of the United States, and its Protectorates. It is suggested that the President and Vice President run as a team, just as they current do.

"Now the big one; the current the Senate will be replaced by a new division of representation and responsibility, which will be the Senate of American Republics.

"And the House of Representatives will be replaced by a Citizens Parliament."

Attorney General Nevins hand flipped up as he asked, "Like England?"

"Sort of, Larry, but more like Canada. The British Parliament is burdened with complex relationships with the Royalty and the House of Lords, which are hereditary, not elected. We will have none of that.

"What is being suggested for our new government is three separate levels of governance, each level dealing with those matters most relevant with a certain segment of the national body.

"This is modeled on our court system; but different, of course. Our Supreme Court adjudicates matters affecting the nation; the Superior Court system operates on a state level; and Municipal Courts operate on county and city level.

Althea Johnson, Secretary of Treasury raises her hand and asks, "Woody, we don't have Republics, we have states. I read ahead a little way and it suggests that 'Republics are a group of States, and States are groups of Districts. Where does all of this come from?"

"Good question, Althea. We have to create them; and it won't be easy. What the report called 'Districts used to be called counties. And counties are a group of precincts."

"Not easy you say," Althea interjects, "We are going to need your Army, Navy, ... and your Air Force to make that kind of change!"

"Understood, Althea; let's include the Coast Guard, too. We are looking forward, expecting considerable resistance, especially at the precinct level.

"But let me remind you, every ten years there is a national census of the population; and the boundaries' of the precincts are re-drawn by the governments of the states in which they are located. Political parties, representing only the rich and powerful individuals and companies, have had a banquet in their States for too long, while working class starves on table scraps.

"Althea, that is absolutely unacceptable. We are going to make it impossible for the rich and powerful to have the ability to Gerrymander the precincts. That is going to end. They will no longer able to have a neighborhood with one vote representing twenty of the rich, and across town, another neighborhood, with one vote representing five thousand of the poor.

"Oh shit," Althea Johnson mumbled as she fingered the edge of her copy of the report.

The President pauses for a moment and then continues, "Althea, you were a ball of cleansing fire before we were elected; this is your opportunity re-ignite that fire; the National Census Bureau, is part of the Treasury Department.

After a deep sigh Secretary Johnson says, "I hear you, Mister President; and I thank you. I lost sight of our end game for a moment. But I'm going to need a lot more manpower and womanpower."

"You'll have it. One of my major goals is to kill the Gerrymander beast and bury it so deep that the fires of hell will feast on it."

"The President pauses for a moment, takes a drink of water and then says, "Just before this meeting I was informed by the Republic Formation Committee that they have a first draft of the geographic boundaries and names of the proposed Republics and Protectorates. They are the same as they were in the initial draft; no change; eight Republics and three Protectorates.

"It is still a work in progress and this may change. I have ordered copies sent to your electronics"

A few moments later the President while looking at his monitor says, "There it is; that is the Commonwealth of American Republics."

"Secretary Cortez asks, "Why did they chop up Florida? When did New York City become a State?"

"Yesterday; maybe this morning, Bob."

"Why?"

"Ask the committee, Bob. Put it in writing, send an e-mail. They are still in session trying to figure out the details of the powers and authority of the Republics."

"And how to pay for all of this, I hope."

"That's right, Bob."

Chris Donovan, Heimdall's clerk, comes bustling through the door and goes straight to the President and hands him a note.

After a quick glance at the note Heimdall announces, "I'm sorry, this is a matter requiring immediate attention, we will adjourn until tomorrow, same time.

"Morgan, Sullivan; I need a few moments."

The Secretaries of State and Defense sat back down.

Chief of Staff Dumont ushers the other cabinet members out and shuts the door.

The President begins, "As you know, the Government of Iran is blaming the United States for the disappearance of one of their ships.   They are raising hell and vowing to get revenge; to answer in kind.

"It's absurd, our fleet in the Arabian Sea hasn't fired a shot, it isn't even on alert."

"This note is from General Porter; he is in the Pentagon War right now.   He informs me that what looks like the entire Iranian Navy is on alert and moving.   Two destroyers and a fleet of accompanying gunboats are moving towards the Arabian Sea.

"General Porter is tired of their bull shit; I am tired of their bull shit; the American people are tired of their bullshit! Unless you can come up with a good reason to ignore this threat and back down, again, I'm going to issue the orders for our carrier, the Gerald Ford, and its fleet, to proceed to the Arabian Sea and prepare for combat."

After a short moment of silence Secretary of State, Charles Morgan asks, "Are you leaving open any paths for negotiation?"

"Not as yet, but you need to set up contacts for possible negotiations.

"I will need some time.'"

"How much will you need?"

"As much as you can give me. Remember, it is approaching noon here; It is approaching midnight in most of Europe."

"Okay, Morgan; let's see. When our fleet begins to move the world will notice. Within one hour all major military powers will wonder what we are doing. We will maintain radio silence and answer no questions. By the second hour of our fleet being underway the Iranian government should be in a state of panic, they will have a good idea what we can do to them if they really piss us off. This is what we hope for."

"That gives you two hours to notify our allies that we have no intentions beyond stopping the harassment of our ships in the Arabian Sea. But we will return fire if interfered with. Can you do that?"

"Oh, yes. I will contact England, France, Italy and Japan first and ask that they relay the message to all their allies. That should do it."

"What about Russia and China."

"No need, their espionage systems usually pass information as fast as our diplomatic channels do."

"They will probably call you, Woody."

The President chuckles; "You think? And, like the bad boy after a bad first date, I won't answer."

Morgan chuckles, "Really Woody; and I thought you were a gentleman."

"Morgan, like all successful politicians in this world, beneath my persona of dignity, honesty and openness there is a fully developed scoundrel seeking influence, power, and control in order to put things the 'right way' as I see them.

"Fortunately, a lot of us have good intentions, most of the time."

Woody laughs, "Two hours, Charly, two hours."

British Prime Minister, Carlyle Hastings is in the process of muttering every profanity he knows as he puts on his slippers and robe. He gets to his bedroom desk, switches on the smart phone and shouts, "This had better be God damned important or you should prepare yourself to serve the remainder of your enlistment at our station in Antarctica.

The folds and creases in his face seem to sag further as he watches the report on the phone.

"Have you tried all channels?" He asks.

"Yes, Sir. None of our allies have any explanations, or even information. The Americans are maintaining radio and satellite silence. But our satellites show the Carrier Fleet is moving toward the Arabian Sea at thirty knots. That's battle speed, Sir."

"I know that is battle speed, God damn it! Major, keep on it and keep me posted at this number, it is my home office. We are not going on full alert just because one naïve, stupid, arrogant, egotistic American teenager wants to play a game of War."

"Yes Sir."

"Just keep me posted."

"Yes Sir."

"And you never heard me say those things about the American president; understand?"

"Yes Sir. Completely Sir."

Hastings puts down the phone and begins to pace around the large bedroom apparently deep in thought.

A servant brings in a cup of tea and some cakes.

Hastings glances and tea and cakes; as the servant leaves, he murmurs, "Thank you."

He is thinking, I can't reach General Porter; I can't reach President Heimdall, I can't reach anyone in the diplomatic service in America. All our allies are in the same position. America is silent and no one has means to get any information except for what our satellites see.

But to do nothing might result in losing he initiative if a war starts. To go on alert might goad some other nation to begin hostilities.

I don't know, I don't know, I just don't know!

But America and the United Kingdom have been the closest of allies for a century and a half now; our cultures, our values and beliefs are the same. And we have always prevailed when we worked in unison.

He shouts as he turns toward his desk, "God damn the adolescent, testosterone driven bravado of that American! He behaves like the Royalty of eighteenth-century Europe. We gave up wars; except for the Napoleonic wars, the Colonial wars, World War One, the Russian

Revolution, World War Two, the Southeast Asian Wars, all the African revolutions, … … and … Oh, to hell with it."

The Prime Minister strides back to his desk and takes out a red smart phone and punches in a code. The face plate lights up. He texts "Area eleven; battle ready; level …' he pauses for moment, then texts 'three."

He puts the phone back in the desk drawer, sits down, and begins to eat one of his cakes. He is thinking, Level three may cost a lot but it will keep our troops on United Kingdom soil. I don't trust this Yank President and his 'kick ass' attitude, but somehow, someway we English speaking nations will prevail and prosper.

□ □ □ □ □ □

□ □ □ □ □

Department of Interior Secretary, Roberto Cortez asks, "Any news from the battlefront yet?"

President Heimdall replies, "Only that there is no battle front yet. The satellites show that there are planes on the Gerald Ford's flight deck, gun covers have been removed from all weapon systems and the fleet speed has increased to forty knots.

When the carrier turns into the wind the planes will pop off those decks like swarms of locusts."

Cortez smiles at the thought about the Presidents last comment. He offers, hornets than lLocusts; Sir."

The President nods an says, "You got that right; angry hornets, with deadly stingers."

The President relaxes some and continues, "Communication silence works both ways, Roberto. Our incoming information is limited to what the satellites and drones can see.

"Fleet Admiral Zygier is on his own."

"Any idea when we might know something?"

"Nope. Let's get back to what the Department of Interior has accomplished so far. "

"Okay. We now have a Water Rights and Ownership Bureau along with the newly created Court of Mineral Assets in the Department of the Interior; they are up and running; waiting for your order to proceed on our first assignment.

"For what purpose?" Heimdall asks.

"This will create flexibility for what we are really going to investigate, ownership of water and mineral rights. Local wars have persisted since first Europeans set foot on this continent.

"Water from underground aquifers is now on the verge of disappearing within the next few decades. The 'fracking for oil' process is poisoning the remaining ground water.

"We intend to investigate all decisions by Federal courts where preservation of ground water is part of the question. This will be an omnibus order starting with the most recent decisions and rolling back as far as court decisions are available.

"Our biggest problem will be the oil companies; they could tie us up in court for decades, or until the country runs out of drinking water."

"And do you have a proposal to solve this problem?"

"We do, Woody. We need a Presidential Order declaring ground water as an endangered asset, critical to the survival of the nation and its population. And an order prohibiting any further fracking."

Woody looks at Chief of staff, Lorraine Dumont.

She shrugs and says, "It makes sense to me. Of course, we will have to kill a few thousand oil company executives. But, what the hell, they breed like rabbits wherever they smell oil."

"Get serious Lorraine, what will be the biggest problem?"

"State governments in the northern plains. You have a war about to start in Asia, you don't need one in the Dakotas, too."

Roberto interjects, "Buy some time. Declare a one-week halt of fracking while we investigate a potential danger. With the help of federal officers, we can drag that out until we can develop a strategy."

"Let's give it a try. Do you have a draft of the orders?"

As he takes a folder out of his brief case he grins and answers, "Yeah, I just happen to have one with me."

He extends the folder to the President who says, "Give it to Chris, he will prepare the formal document."

As Chris gets up to get the document Lorraine asks, "Would you like some help with that?"

Chris smiles, "Two sets of eyes are usually better than one."

The President comments, "I want to sign that tomorrow morning and release it to the press by the afternoon.

Chris nods his head; Lorraine quietly says, "Tyrant."

The President says, "Let's break for lunch."

After lunch another cabinet member joins the group, Attorney General: Lawrence Nevins.

President Heimdall welcomes him and says, "Glad you could join us, Larry, we are going through the list of urgent matters that have been targeted to be changed by Presidential Orders.

"Thanks, Woody, I have the rest of the afternoon at your disposal. I have a dinner meeting with some Governor's regarding changes to the judicial systems."

The President continues," You have before you my order that all immigration from Mexico and Central American will cease except for diplomats, international businessmen and those with green cards.

"All seasonal workers green cards must be renewed yearly. All other foreign visitors, for whatever reasons, may apply for 'permits' for a certain limited amount of time. The permits may be renewable and/or extended but that requires a new application.

"Any questions, complaints, suggestions or modifications?

There were none; Heimdall continues, "Very well.

He passes the document across the table to his clerk, Chris.

Heimdall continues, "You will love the next one; I am temporarily banning the sales of automatic firing rifles and extended ammunition clip hand guns to individuals until an investigation has been completed.

"Violation of this order will be a felony and will result in penalties and/or jail time.

"Sale to approved militaries and law enforcement groups are not banned.

"This ban includes sales by any and all American and foreign manufacturers, retail and/or wholesale stores, agents, political organizations, gun clubs, citizen posse's, public or private museums, or private citizens. "Any questions, complaints, suggestions or modifications?"

No one says a word.

Heimdall asks, "No one? I'll be damned; I expected and hour or two of arguments."

Nevins states, "This is not Texas, Montana or Alaska, that is where you will get your arguments."

"I guess so; Chris, take care of this, please

Chris is grinning as he accepts the folder.

Heimdall continues, "Well, let's see how much conversation this one generates; Women's Health.

"I am temporally declaring that adequate health services are a right guaranteed by the original Constitution and Bill of Rights of the United States of America.

"I am taking this action now to establish that the phrase 'adequate services' includes a women's reproduction organs; and that includes abortion, if requested.

"This order will seriously limit the ability of States to deny abortions to women who want them.

"It will also, postpone court actions until the New Constitution is completed, enacted and operating.

"Are there any questions, complaints, suggestions or modifications?"

Silence prevailed for a long moment, then Chief of Staff, Lorrain Dumont began to applaud, then the others in the room joined in.

The doors burst open and the two guards rushed in and stared around with confused looks on their faces.

President Heimdall stands up and extends the folder to Chris Donovan, who bows as he excepts the draft of the Presidential Order.

The guards shake their heads and return to their posts outside the doors.

Just as the doors were about to close an Army Captain comes running down the hall, through the doors and goes directly to President Heimdall.

□□□□□□ □□□□□□□

President Heimdall stands silently by a window looking at the flower garden outside. Everyone else is also silent, waiting for the President to speak. He finally turns away from the window and quietly but clearly says, "Well, we all knew it was inevitable, didn't we? We hoped it wouldn't happen, but we knew ... we knew it would happen. That is the reason we created the ORB response."

The President's voice and confidence rose as he continued. "ORB has ten levels; we have been setting at level 2 ever since the election; General Porter is waiting for me to give the order to initiate a Level 7 response. That level is designed to destroy the ability of foes to launch a counter response. Civilians are not targeted although many will be killed due to collateral damage.

"I see no cause to delay an ORB 7 response, perhaps one or more of you do; feel free to speak up."

There was no response, all those in the room remain silent.

The President turns to the Army Officer and says, "Captain, would you please read the first paragraph again; slowly and loudly.

"Sir; Yes Sir!" he shouts. "Three freighters were fired upon and sunk in the South China Sea. Two were registered as Filipino; one was British. The accompanying American patrol ships were also fired upon. One destroyer was sunk, another destroyer and a battle cruiser suffered significant damage. The attacking fleet consisted of one Chinese Cruiser, several coastal patrol ships and an unknown number of submarines, Sir!"

President Heimdall asks, "Did General Porter send any message to us about his readiness?

"He did, Sir! He said, 'We are ready! ORB 7 is ready; locked, loaded and awaiting orders, Sir!"

"Thank you, Captain."

"There's more, Sir!"

"Go ahead."

"General Porter said nine submarines are on station, armed and ready. Two carrier fleets are moving at top speed toward the China coast; one to the East China Sea, north of Taiwan; the other to the South China Sea. That's all, Sir!"

The President looks at the others in the room and asks "Any second thoughts?" No one answers.

"None? Good; I have none either.

"Lorraine, contact General Porter on the 'urgent' line; tell him you are speaking for me; that I have signed the Declaration of War and I am busy with political things. Tell him he is in charge now; commence response in exactly one hour from this second.

"Also, I wish him good hunting. Send them to Hell!"

With a big smile on her face, Lorraine salutes and scurries out of the room."

Heimdall looks around, Attorney General Nevins and the Captain are the only ones left in the room.

Heimdall chuckles and questions, out loud, "I wonder if our allies have been notified?"

Nevins offers, "I could check that out for you."

"Thanks, Nevins; but no thanks; Chris will be back in a few minutes and he will take care of it, if he hasn't already done it. It is part of our drill for an ORB emergency.

"If a war starts my clerk immediately informs the State Department; they will notify the rest of the world.

"The Chinese government and militaries have one last hour to survive."

"I'm sure Japan, South Korea, and Great Britain have already noticed our mobilization; I'm sure they have already correctly guessed and notified their assets in the region.

"Is there anything else, Nevins?"

"Just one thing; is the use of tactical nuclear weapons still not an option."

"Correct."

"Even with North Korea?'
"Correct; without China the Kim regime won't last three weeks. We are going to re-unify Korea, we don't want the north to be radioactive.

□□□□□□□

□□□□□□□□

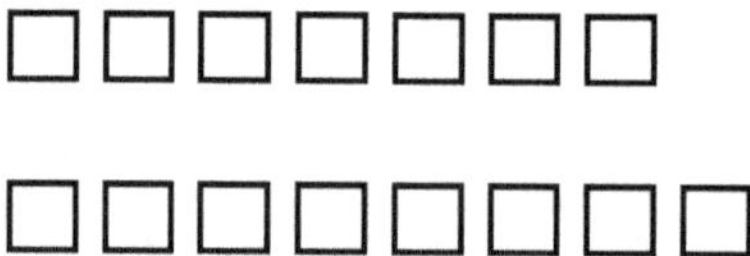

Breaking News:
War in South China Sea

Reliable foreign sources reported that earlier today, in the South China Sea, nine American nuclear-powered submarines rose to the surface. For the next two hours Chinese military ports and other strategic costal locations were bombarded by Cruise Missiles.

An American Declaration of War with China was posted on worldwide internets *half an hour before the bombardment began.*

The Chinese naval fleets wherever they were became aware that they were under surveillance, , by American 'sleeper subs' armed with armor penetrating torpedoes, and had been for a long time. All four of the Chinese Carriers were sunk or are burning along with numerous other naval vessels.

Attempts to contact anyone in the United States Government's Administration has been unsuccessful.

All military bases, forts, ports, offices, and other facilities answer questions with the same recorded message. "Due to a national emergency all military communication is silenced for an unknown period of time.

They are not accepting messages.

More news to follow when it is available.

President Heimdall is sitting alone in the Oval Office; he adjourned the Cabinet Meeting and sent his aide, Chris, on a long break. The President wanted to be alone as he viewed and listened to the military reports on his tablet.

He had on earphones and he felt as if he was there, part of the action. He was living the event; he didn't want others to know of his passion for war movies, especially those about World War Two. He could sit for hours 'experiencing' movies or TV series like 'Patton', 'Midway', 'Band of Brothers', 'Platoon' and others.

His wife and children didn't seem to care, but the voters might have some reservations about having a President whose favorite diversion was to become immersed in war movies.

Sometimes Woodrow Heimdall worried about that himself; but not for long. Although he has never worn a uniform, he a warrior to get thing done.

Breaking News:

War in North China Sea

A reliable source *is reporting that an American Carrier Fleet assigned to the North China Sea has arrived in its' area of* *operation and is in action. The fleet's stealth fighter/bombers are attacking inland targets as hyper-sonic fighters clear the way.*

Our source is a Bengali journalist, in Beijing; he states that the Chinese capital has experienced massive destruction and is on fire. We have no confirming evidence, but satellites show a smoke storm over the area.

Additional News: The American Carrier Fleet Assigned to protect Taiwan has arrived on station and commenced their mission. Any vessel at sea that is identified as Chinese military will be sunk.

Also, American fighter bombers are devastating military ships and suspected military ships in the ports. This information is from a source in Taiwan; it is considered reliable but not yet confirmed.

Stay tuned for further as it becomes available.

"The order came; the order was obeyed; that is all there is to it. I closed the Market; locked down the electronics; and now I'm going to take a short vacation; and enjoy it."

Oscar Franklin Deming has a loud voice for such a short man. He is only five foot six inches tall, thin and wiry build; but he is Chairman of the New York Stock Exchange; which makes him the biggest gorilla on Wall Street.

There is another peculiar thing about Frank Deming, he is only fifty-four years old. Chairmen of the New York Stock Exchange have almost always been white men in their sixties or seventies.

"Thanks, Frank. I sure hope all goes as you predicted."

"It will, Woody. There will be some unexpected collateral damage, but nothing a few emergency loans after the lock down can't fix.

"The markets will open, cash will start flowing and everything will return to as it, except China will be missing.

"Also, the world economy will be better off without that bunch of economic criminals."

"Well thank you Frank. As always, I feel better after discussing my problems with you.

"Enjoy your vacation."

Most of Deming's associates consider him a 'bully; Woody Heimdall considers him a friend; a trusted friend.

Off stage, behind the scenes, Frank Deming is Woody Heimdall's economic advisor and mentor.

Woody is only a multi-billionaire; Frank became a multi-trillionaire many years ago.

They share an encrypted, personal and private phone line.

The President disconnects his line to the Chairman and sits for a moment, drumming his fingers on the desk top. He is thinking about what he has just ordered.

He says to himself, I sure hope Frank is right about all this. He says that closing every major economy on Earth at the same time, for one forty-eight-hour period will cause a 'global reset.'

Forty-eight hours. At first there will be global panic; all commerce will freeze due to a lack of liquidity of the currencies of the world; everything stops. Then everyone will look for ways to protect what wealth they have left. Then they will see that all their wealth is leveraged debt; over leveraged debt; way overleveraged debt.

The only way commerce will restart is when the governments with the largest economies cooperate with each other to restore international liquidity of all currencies.

These nations will have placed economic pistols to their own heads. They can pull the trigger, destroy the world's economies, which will annihilate about eighty percent of the Earth's population and throw civilization back to about where it was in the tenth century AD.

They won't start agreeing and cooperating with each other for a couple of days; then fear will drive them together.

All nations can sit down and create a world economy which is neither the bloody claws and fangs of capitalism, nor the bleeding-heart incompetence of socialism.

He wonders; maybe we humans can create a world economy that rewards competency, skill and creativity, that also provides basic services and commodities for all citizens, and also protects essential rights, privileges, opportunities and equality within national law.

This will require laws that recirculate excessive wealth of corporations, companies and individuals back into the general economy to support social services; education institutions; medical services; protection from fire, disaster, and criminal activity; and other essential services.

A legal fire wall must be created to separate, politics and government activity. Government must not be a 'for profit' activity.

We really need similar fire wall between government and religions or philosophies. Personal religious belief must not determine law or government operation.

This is impossible at the present time but steps that direction can be taken.

And the practice of discrimination due to gender, ethnicity, race, language, nationality, occupation or career, sexual choice, marital status, and some other social characteristics is disgusting and destructive to social order. It will always be there, but it should not be celebrated or have legal status.

Frank is optimistic that this new civilization will emerge in the next few decades; I'm hopeful some parts of it does.

The President goes back to reading the next recommendations of the Constitution Committee on his desk.

Breaking News
From around the world

Canberra, Australia: *the government announced that the combined armed forces of Australian and New Zealand, protected by a British cruiser fleets landed in the primary ports of New Guinea, and Indonesia, unopposed.*

The Japanese Navy announced that its' military forces are on full alert; and that two of its three carrier fleets are now in the Sea of Japan and occupy positions along the Russian Coast.

Elsewhere; North Korea has threatened nuclear war; South Korea is now on full, combat alert and an undisclosed number of satellites have moved into positions over North Korea.

India is rushing troops and materials north to its borders with China, Russia and Pakistan.

All NATO nations are on military alert, even Switzerland.

Additional News: *A European newsman in Beijing is reporting that there is no remaining government of any sort in the city and suburbs of Beijing. Indeed, there is little of anything remaining undamaged in this city.*

Most of the fires have burned out; most of the buildings which were reinforced concrete and with limited combustibles, remain standing.

With Beijing destroyed and without any central government; provinces, cities, schools, factories and other groups are searching, begging, looking for someone, anyone, to surrender to.

He further reports that survivors are beginning to caravan out of the city toward suburbs and farmlands beyond. Most are walking, leaving the dead and dying behind, on the sides of the roads.

Occasional helicopters drop in to pick up survivors, mostly Europeans and other non-Chinese journalists. He states that his group is scheduled for the next chopper. He states 'he must leave, or face starvation.'

In other war news, the fleet of the carrier Gerald Ford is now in the Arabian Sea and ready for action. It's presence and the actions taken against China and North Korea seam to have had a calming effect on the Iranian government.

Iran's Army and Navy are no longer on battle alert and its navy has returned to the more mundane tasks of shore patrol and cargo inspections.

They rediscovered the peace that can be found in silence.

The President's consort is in her own office in the White House talking to Chief of Staff: Lorrain Dumont.

"I guess this cancels my European Tour."

"Not at all, Celeste, the war has increased the importance of your tour. You are no longer the high-profile White House 'Charmer in Chief,' you are the woman who sleeps with the President every night; you are his closest confidant.

Celest frowns, purses her lips and says, "Well, not every night. You would be surprised how many mornings I wake up alone."

"Perhaps so, but you are no longer just the President's wife, you are his ambassador, his envoy, his face, his voice.

"Every political leader in Europe wants to know what the President is trying to accomplish, what he is thinking, what he is planning. You are the only one close enough to him to know his most intimate thoughts."

"And it had better stay that way;" the President's woman growled.

Lorrain chuckled and continued, "You must stay alert, every politician you meet is trying to get you to slip up and reveal secrets."

"Lorraine, I intend to be discreetly aggressive in my contact with any and all these strutting roosters.

"A smile, a hand placed on someone's arm, a confusing question to change the subject; they are all part of my tool kit. If the going gets tough I can always spill a drink on my cleavage or trip and fall into someone's arms in a compromising manner."

Lorraine chuckles again as says, "Celest, *you are* a diplomat, you will do just fine. We are thinking of changing your schedule to add a few more European capitals. This will increase your time spent in Europe to three weeks."

"I'll have to ask the Boss."

"I already did; he approved it."

"Are my children going on the full trip."

"Yes, your kids are going with you, too."

"I'm going to tell the Boss you called his children 'kids."

"Please don't."

"Okay, but watch that."

"Okay; are we okay?"

"We're okay.
"Okay."

<u>Breaking News</u>
<u>From around the world</u>

The Pentagon released a statement this morning that in South Korea two army divisions have moved north across the cease fire zone, and continuing North.   One division is South Korean; the other American.

Following the combat troops in each Division is a caravan of supply trucks. The caravans are huge, assembling at points up to a hundred miles back in South Korea.

Attached to each division are several Military Field Hospitals, Engineering Battalions, Military Police and Civilian Affairs Companies.

Also, a convoy of about thirty cargo ships is in the Korea Sea, escorted by six South Korean destroyers. These supply ships are enroute to Nampo, North Korea's largest seaport.

Inland, a Korean/American air lift of food and other supplies is about to begin. As the armies proceed north liberating small airports, each airfield will become a destination site for light cargo and passenger planes carrying needed supplies and personnel.

By mid-winter almost all of North Korea should be supplied with food and fuel and working on the details of re-unification of the North and South.

It appears that a bloodless coupe occurred in Pyongyang. The Kim family has disappeared. It is believed they have fled the country.

The leaders of the coupe have contacted the South Korean Army and said their local Home Guard has taken control of Pyongyang and are waiting in place to surrender.

More news to follow as it becomes available.

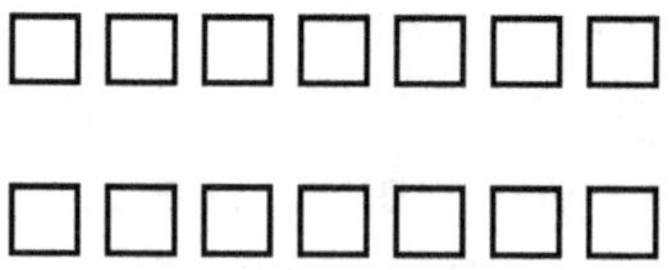

There is no response from America.
Days go by; a week, more days
The world Is holding its' breath; waiting for the next American response.
Suddenly, with no advance notice, it is there, on the internet. It is a brief and simple series of statements.

The United States of America declares a 'cease fire.' It begins immediately.   Its' military will not occupy any portion of China. We will participate in the creation of a protectorate under the jurisdiction of the United Nations.

The 'New China' will surrender or destroy all nuclear weapons and the means of constructing such weapons.

Taiwan will become an independent nation, and a member of the United Nations.

There has not been, and will not be, a change in the position of the United States.

Every nation where the United States of America has a diplomatic office receives the same message.

Another week goes by, Russia and all its' puppet states file charges in every international court that has any jurisdiction. They do not declare war but label the United State of America a rogue state

They put all their military on full scale alert and warn that they will use nuclear weapons to protect the rest of the world if America does not de-escalate the hostilities.

A day after the American message, there is an e-message from the nation of India to all members of the United Nations. It offers to host a cease fire conference concerning the China question, in Mumbai.

After a week of haggling, the United States of America, Great Britain, India, Russia, and Japan agree to meet in The Hague, Netherlands.   Other nations are invited to attend but will have no vote.

In his office President Heimdall smiles. The American government remains silent, but ceases bombardment of the Chinese military facilities.

But all is not quiet and peaceful in the rest of the world. Almost all major armies cease firing and stand in place; but random guerilla armies and other small combat units do not.

There are no further words or actions from America. Almost everywhere soldiers relax, some even talk with opposing soldiers; they ask questions, tell stories and show each other pictures of their families.

None talk of the killing that could start again, at any moment.

Meanwhile, as foreign assistance and trade with China ceases to exist, so does China's ability to provide food and health services to its' citizens. Starvation and disease began killing millions.

North Korea's attempt to launch missiles toward South Korea and Japan proved to be fruitless. The American Navy had deployed umbrellas of anti-missile drones over all their launch sites. Only a few managed to rise more than a hundred yards before exploding. Most exploded as they emerged from their launch silos. The North Korean Missile Force destroyed itself.

The few missiles that managed a successful launch were taken out by navel aircraft.

The Kim family escaped the military coup that followed the attempted war. After a fruitless search to find a safe haven the Kim family bought themselves asylum in Gabon, Africa.

That only lasted a while; the entire family was executed a few months after they fled Korea.

During the decades of the tyrannical Kim régime the quality and reliability of the civil services and administration plummeted.

There were very few who could run a parking lot, let alone a government department. North Korean had to rely on South Korea, Japan, the United States to reestablish an operating nation.

The United States longest war, the United States verses North Korea, came to an end when a United Nations Resolution declared that Korea was now one nation.

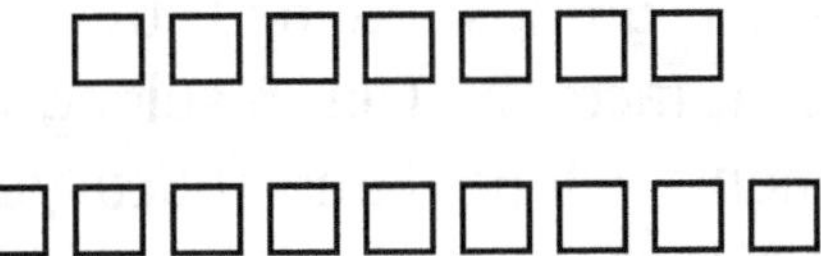

At the 'China Administration Conference' at the Hague, Russia's consistent 'no' vote becomes irrelevant. The bloc consisting of the United States of America, the United Kingdom of Great Britain, India, and Japan dictate the terms and conditions of the agreement being negotiated.

The first article passed and enacted is that whatever remains of the local city and state governments will remain in positions as they now exist, and continue their duties and responsibilities.

Existing authorities, cultures, languages and religions are recognized and will continue with their duties and practices.

The Communist Party is banned and all or its executives placed under temporary house arrest.

These executives will continue their duties but be subordinate to and monitored by the China Administration Conference.

Cities and states will be re-organized as regional groups defined by geography and social factors. The resulting Regional Governments will be democratically elected.

A National Government will be formed and will be democratically elected by Representatives of the Regional Governments.

Any attempts to re-establish The Communist Party will be regarded as a Crime against humanity and treated accordingly.

The Economy will be reorganized on a mixed socialist/capitalist model. Essential services will be government controlled and operated.

The remainder of the economy will embrace capitalism but will be closely monitored by government agencies.

Corporations, trusts and similar economic agencies will not have special benefits or considerations before the law.

Primary officers, boards of directors and others in decision making positions will be held personally accountable for violation of civil, criminal, economic, ecological, and humanitarian laws.

Reasonable reparations from private or corporate funds may be considered.

Various Northern European economic models will be studied.

Russia objected, refused to sign and withdrew from the Conference.

The world began to re-group into four major blocs: United States of America and its' Western hemisphere allies; North Atlantic Treaty Organization; Russia and its' Central Asia allies; and the uncommitted nations. The major players in the uncommitted bloc are India, Japan, Brazil, Indonesia, Saudi Arabia, Nigeria, Egypt, and Israel.

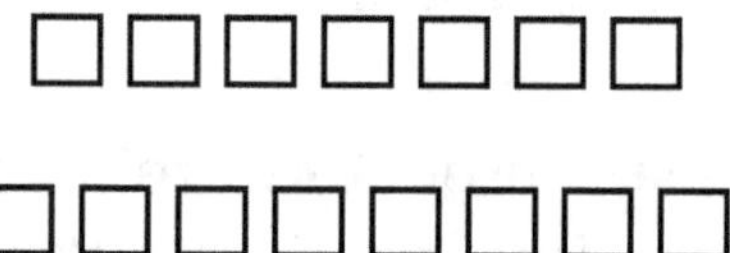

The Cabinet is in session but the President has not yet arrived. Secretary of the Treasury, Althea Johnson asks, "Are we in session for the President to declare that we won the war?"

"No one wins a war; it is a question of who loses the most." Secretary of State: Charles Morgan answers. "The one who loses the least gets to dictate the terms and conditions of survival to the ones who lost the most."

"But only for a few decades." Secretary of Defense, Forest Sullivan interjects. "The definition of 'peace' is that period of time between wars. That period ends when the 'Big Dog' from the previous war loses its dominance over the 'Little Dogs' in the neighborhood. Then, alone, or as a pack, the 'Little Dogs' decide they can whip the 'Big Dog.'

"It never ends," Interior Secretary Cortez says. "It is a human disease; war goes on forever."

"Cain slew Abel, that's what started it all;" Secretary Sullivan says.

Secretary Cortez replies, "Oh, so now we are going to blame 'God?'"

"Yak, yak, yak; I'm glad I am a Buddhist. Secretary Morgan states. Dharma is, and it is beyond human understanding, comprehension, or description; but we do, experience it. No one knows how or why; we just know we can."

"So why don't we just shut up and live in the moment?" Cortez asks

President Heimdall comes into the room, he pauses and states, "Stay seated, we have work to do.

"I heard that last sentence and agree with it; and in *this moment* we have a couple of Presidential Orders to discuss, critique and modify where needed.

"Then we have the report from the Constitution Committee to review."

He begins to read from the tablet in his hand, "First; I have ordered a ban on ownership and/or possession of military style automatic rifles by civilians. All these weapons are to be turned over to Federal, State, County or Municipal offices within thirty days from the signing of this order.

"Failure to comply with this order is a felony and will result in arrest and prosecution by local law enforcement agencies."

The President glances over the top of the tablet in his hands, then he continues, "

"Charges for those arrested will be adjudicated in the Superior Court System of the State in which the crime was committed.

Penalties for committing these felonies will be as follows."

He glances at the Cabinet members again, and then continues:

"Possession of an illegal weapon; two to five years, of federal, or local incarceration.

"Sale of weapons; five to ten years; Federal incarceration.

"Aiding and abetting sale or possession of weapons; five to ten years; Federal incarceration.

"Injury or wounding someone with this type of weapon; five to twenty years; Federal incarceration.

Murder or manslaughter with these types of weapons; life incarceration; no parole available except for those with a terminal disease or injury: or those above the age of sixty years."

There are gasps around the table.

The President holds up a hand and says, "No questions or arguments, please.

After a short pause he continues, "No civilized nation can allow the presence or operation of private armies within their borders; and maintain civil law and order.

"The Second Amendment to the Original Constitution, as discussed in the Federalist Papers, clearly indicates that the Founding Fathers were protecting the rights of settlers to hunt for game, and/or to defend themselves from criminal acts and raids by hostile Native American warriors.

"The only weapons in use at that time were single shot, muzzle loading rifles shotguns and handguns. This order does not ban standard shotguns, hunting rifles or revolvers; *it bans automatic loading guns!*

"The Founding Fathers never heard of, or dreamed of, God damned machine guns!

"The Second Amendment in the Bill of Rights was approved two hundred years before functional automatic weapons were invented.

"The Founding Fathers would never have approved of a citizen's right to mass slaughter other citizens.

"The removal of this type of weapon from the general public will go a long way in stopping the mass murder of innocent citizens, by deranged individuals, which has plagued our country for the last century.

"It is a certainty that the next Supreme Court will be quite busy with complaints about the order.

"So be it!" Let the courts decide!"

After a short pause the President clears his throat and then continues, "The next Presidential Order suspends issuing any further permits to use the 'fracking' procedure to secure oil and natural gas.

Existing permits will be honored for sixty days. This will allow the oil and gas drilling companies time to phase out the use of the 'fracking' procedure.

"Failure to comply will result in the Department of the Interior shutting down all operations of the company violating the order."

The President looks up and restates, "I mean, *all operations; everywhere! including pipelines*"

The President pauses for a moment and then says, "Well I'm sure I have given you plenty to think about, and I am sure you are itching to talk to each other. So, let us take a long lunch break and reconvene at two o'clock to go through the report from the Constitution Committee.

"Dismissed."

The Cabinet Members are all in their seats by two o'clock and the President is right on time. All the Cabinet Members start to stand up.

Heimdall frowns, slaps his papers down on the table and growls, "Sit down; and stop doing that! This is not a Monarchy, nor is it a worship service; we are just a bunch of citizens temporarily given the responsibility of running this government!"

Everyone sits down rather quickly. The President begins, "You're copies of the report is on the table. Let's take five minutes for you to scan the report, then we can discuss it section by section.

"But before we begin with that, I would like to answer a question I have been asked several times, "How secure are these meetings?"

"Well, the US Army has established defense lines around the White House, major federal government buildings in the District of Columbia, and the Pentagon across the river. These lines are manned by regular Army Infantry, twenty-four seven. Their weapons are loaded.

"Drones are also over the protected areas; also, on station twenty-four seven. And a lot of those little devils are 'Hunter-Killers,' searching for *illegal* drones which don't have the day's user code.

"And then there are about twelve hundred soldiers on level three alert within fifteen minutes of the capital.

"The Coast Guard is patrolling the Potomac River; and everyone who wears a military uniform knows who we are, where we are, and what we are doing.

"Now back to this report.

"The Constitution Committee is composed of scholars in the fields of Constitutional Law, American History, American Society, and American Economics. Each was nominated by one or more off the Presidents of twenty-four highly reputed American Universities."

"There is an addendum to the report containing the profiles of the Committee members. You can read those on your own and bring up any complaints at our next meeting.

"Now we have a presentation prepared for us."

The twelve-foot-wide television screen on the back wall lights up and soft background music comes out of the speakers as the document appears.

Overview

Congress and Executive

It is strongly suggested by the Committee that the new government adopt a constitution closely following what is presented in the following text.

You will notice that it consists of modified, updated and clarified statements drawn from the founding documents of the Canadian Parliament and United States Congress.

The House of Commons will consist of representatives elected by a vote of the citizens of each Region. There will be two (2) representatives per Region.

For election purposes, the nation is divided into fifty (50) Regions, with two thousand (2,000) Districts per Region; with one thousand, five hundred (1,500) Precincts per District; and approximately five hundred (500) Voters per Precinct.

The boundaries of these Regions, Districts and Precincts will be updated and redrawn by the Department of Census once every ten (10) years. The Department of Census will be part of the Department of the Interior.

The practice of Gerrymandering is forbidden. A Court of Census will be created and made part of the Supreme Court System Lower Division. The ten-year census, the redrawn boundary maps, and complaints will be adjudicated in this Court of Census.

The Court will consist of five Justices, each and every one appointed by the sitting President of the United States and approved by a majority vote of the United States Senate.

The history of Nominees will be investigated by the Federal Bureau of Investigated and presented to the United States Senate.

The term of office of Census Court Justices will be for life but not to exceed age sixty-nine (69). Justices may retire at any age they choose. Justices may be impeached by a two thirds majority of the House of Commons.

The House may call for a vote of 'No Confidence' of the Sitting President by a two-thirds majority vote of the House members. If impeachment proceeds, the Senate will sit in judgement of the vote, two weeks after the 'No Confidence' vote.

If the 'no confidence' vote stands the Vice President ascends to the Presidency and a new National Election must be scheduled within two months of the impeachment.

Each of the regions will have two (2) representatives in the House of Commons. The term of office is two (2) years.   No Member of the House of Commons may hold office for more than fifteen (15) consecutive terns (30 years).

Former Members of the House of Commons wishing to return to the House of Commons must wait two terms (4 years) before they can run for election.

No Member of the House of Commons may occupy their position past the age of sixty-nine (69).

Full disclosure of tax records, medical records; and membership in social, business or recreational, clubs or organizations, et cetera will be submitted to and reviewed by the Court of Continuity and Conscience. It is mandatory that this review be completed before selectees are seated in the House or Senate.

The House will initiate all legislation in the following matters: The national budget, local taxation, civil rights, environment protection, public health, education, communication systems, transportation systems and other matters of local or regional importance

The Senate will consist of two (2) representatives, from each state, appointed by the Governor of the state they represent. The residency of the candidate in the State to be represented must have commenced at least four (4) years before the declaration of candidacy is filed.

The term of office is for six (6) years; Senators are limited to three terms (18) years. There is to be a three-year offset between the terms of the two (2) Senators; resulting in the election of one Senator every three years.   No Senator may represent their State after the age of sixty-nine.

Candidates must be at least thirty (30) years of age on the date of seating.

When a seat is vacated for any reason; retirement, limit of term, death debilitating disease, injury or condition, the Governor of the State represented must fill that seat within sixty (60) days or the President of the United States will select a replacement.

The Senate will initiate all legislation concerning foreign relations, foreign trade, international emergencies, international space operations and other matters of global concern and action.

Senators will have no authority or jurisdiction over matters delegated to the House of Commons or the Executive Department of the nation.

House of Commons Representatives will have no authority or jurisdiction over matters delegated to the Senate or the Executive Department of the nation.

The Executive Department may veto any matter passed by both the House and the Senate. Vetoes may be overridden by two thirds vote of the House of Commons.

Presidential Declarations of Emergency and Orders may not be overridden.

The Offices of the President and Vice President will be determined by the results of an election held every four (4) years. Results will be determined by simple majority vote of qualified voters of the national population. The candidates for President and Vice President run for office as a team, not independently.

As the music stops and the picture fades President Heimdall comments, "How about that, I think I understand most of it; how about the rest of you?"

Lorrain Dumont comments, "It looks a lot like the Congress we are used to, but cleaner and leaner and smaller is size; with the addition of a 'no confidence' clause, just in case something gets screwed up."

Treasury Secretary Althea Johnson grins as she states, "I see a real opportunity to save a few billion dollars here, and a few billion dollars there; and if we work at it, we might just save a whole lot of real money. "And just think of all the office space that would open up.

"But it might cause a recession in the restaurant, bars, night club, cab service businesses.

"Why the news reporting and analyzing business alone must generate billions of dollars in payrolls."

Lorrain asks, "And what about the lobbyists, Althea?"

"Oh, Lorrain, there's no such thing as lobbyists, just ask any one of them, they'll all tell you the same thing."

Still grinning Lorrain adds, "I've heard that rumor. That's too bad. Almost everyone I have drinks with wants to make me a very rich. I don't know why."

"Hm, they seem like such nice people. I wonder where all that money comes from?"

Althea wonders out loud, "Come to think of it, I wonder, how much it cost to make that presentation we just saw … writers, directors, sound engineers, caterers, dozens of assistants, hmm …"

President Heimdall raises both hands and loudly says, "The movie breaks over, but we have a little time left."

In just a few moments everyone is back in their seats and waiting for what the President will say next.

He continues, "It appears the Constitution Committee is doing some good work. Think about it overnight and we will discuss modifications at tomorrow's meeting.

"We all noticed the scarcity of details; the Committee is probably waiting for our critique. I suggest that each of us jot down your thoughts before we forget them … because tomorrow … I'm going to submit an idea that will occupy a lot of our time.

"Now, that will give you something to have nightmares about.

He laughs and states, "Dismissed, but don't forget to make those notes on today's presentation.

Breaking News: from around the world!

The world reacts to President Heimdall's banning fracking. The outcry of the oil and gas industry is loud and clear. The President has gone too far!

Most American owned companies begin to *shut down* fracking operations and threaten law suits against the Federal Government.

Almost all non-American owned companies *continue* operations and make threats of law suits.

Great frustration and anger developed when the companies notice that the United States of America doesn't currently have an operating system of courts, and it would take years to get a trial in international courts.

Several foreign based companies refuse to comply; the American State Department advise them that the America government could seize their research operations in America if they don't comply.

Most companies resisting compliance decide to suspend fracking until an agreement could be negotiated.

American stock markets go crazy for a week or so as gasoline prices *rise* about twenty percent.

OPEC nations decide to increase production.

American stock markets go crazy for a week or so as gasoline prices *drop* about twenty percent.

President 'Woody' wins again, for now.

All Cabinet Secretaries, The Chief of Staff, the Attorney General, the Vice President and Colonel Sheila Murphy from the Pentagon are at the meeting. General Porter is still in the Far East.

President Heimdall waits quietly as the conversations quiet down. He glances around the table briefly and then begins, "I wanted to begin our discussion today with Women's rights, especially, women's heath, equality in the workplace, etcetera, but another issue kept nagging at me that it should take priority.

Lorrain Dumont interjects, "Woody, we all had a discussion of your outline of Women's Rights to be protected; health, equal pay for equal work, family leave, freedom from sexual harassment, privacy in locker rooms and toilets and the rest of your list.

Woody looks around and asks, "Are you sure of this; no discussion? "

Lorraine raised her hand and orders, "All in favor of avoiding the umpteenth discussion of what we have all believed In since middle school.!"

All hands shot up.

Monty asks, "Is this some sort of low scale office coup?"

"Not really," Lorrain replies.

"Okay then; how soon can you have the Presidential Order ready?"

Lorraine smiles, "I just happen to have the order here in my satchel."

Without a comment she passes the document around the table to Monty, who signs it and passes it back to Lorrain.

He stretches his shoulders and asks, "How tiring, is there anything else I have nothing to do with, or should we just adjourn?"

"Oh no, Boss. We all want to hear about this idea you are so excited about."

"Well, ookaay, then.

"Most of my adult life I have spent a great deal of time looking at our culture, the American culture and wondering how we survived without even more civil strife than actually occurred.

"I've studied other cultures that have existed for centuries trying to see what it is that bound them together, made them successful.

"Some factors are rather obvious. Before modern transportation geography was the major factor; mountain ranges, large rivers, oceans, deserts, weather, availability of food and water; they all set physical boundaries of cultures.

"Communication is another important factor; our species is a social species; we must communicate with each or our ability to survive diminishes.

"Geographic features separated humans and different groups with different languages developed. Communication became difficult, misunderstandings became common. Prejudice, hostility and conflict were the result of these misunderstandings between cultures.

"The most successful cultures were those which had the most literate and integrated populations. A common language led them to common values, beliefs and commitment to their governments, religions, and social order.

"These values and beliefs were the foundation of nations which prevailed and prospered over their neighbors.

"There is a word, for the what binds a culture together, it is 'Patriotism.'"

President Heimdall pauses for another moment, then resumes his lecture, "The first settlers of the human species in the Americas migrated across a land bridge which connected Asia and North America during the last ice age. Over the centuries these 'First Settlers' dispersed throughout North and South America.

"The settlement of Europeans in North America began with a diverse mixture of explorers from Western European nations; each of which had its' own language; primarily Spanish, French, English, Danish and Portuguese.

'They imposed themselves into the native First Americans, who's populations were already decimated by the European diseases; only small remnants of these people remain in the Americas.

"The success of the first European explorers caught the attention of the rest of Europe and immigrants from the rest of Europe began to arrive.

"Somewhere along the way someone decided that slaves from Africa might be an answer to labor scarcity in America. Once emancipated they became a large minority throughout both North and South America.

"The freedom guaranteed in the American Bill of Rights also brought immigrants from all over the world. This diverse mixture of cultures created the most dynamic culture ever known on this planet.

"But with this diversity and freedom comes division and conflict.

"So, what is it that holds this loud, boiling stew of self-centered individuals together?"

Heimdall pauses for a long moment, and then quietly says, "Patriotism."

He continues, "The belief, the absolute conviction that no matter how flawed, unjust and ugly it gets, what we have here in the United States is better than anything they have anywhere else on Earth."

After a pause the President continues, "This great culture of the United States of American has been slowly rotting at the core for the last hundred and fifty years.

"It is driven by divisive forces of greed, thirst for power, arrogance, ignorance, and the loss of respect for our people, by our people.

President Heimdall pauses for a moment before continuing, "Well' A few weeks ago the American people rose up and demanded change. They didn't elect a president to continue the slow suicide of our country's government, our economy, and our society; they voted for change, for a return to the ideals, visions and promises that have been the character of this nation since its beginning.

"Patriotism is slipping away from them. They don't like it, they won't accept it, they are mad as Hell and won't stand for it!

"*Fix it! Now! They cry.* Give us something to be patriotic about!"

There is a long pause, everyone is quiet. Then Heimdall begins softly, "We have been toying with a lot of ideas; creating and enacting a lot of them. There is one that keeps nagging me; it is radical as Hell, but we are a radical group, in a radical situation.

"Several times in our history, when challenges were grim, the people of the United States have risen up and 'created miracles.'

"Sending Congress home and convening a committee to edit and redact the Constitution of the United States is not a 'miracle,' it is just correcting the maleficence and misconduct of those in office for the last hundred and fifty years.

"Changes in some of our economic procedures are underway; taxation, market practices, banking and insurance, and such. It will all be made public as soon as possible; it is already making a difference.

"But I'm concerned about the *patriotism* of the people, how they view their country.   And I'm looking at what the Administration did in the nineteen thirties to stop the downward spiral of the economy.

"They began a national public works project the likes of which had never been seen before.

"I'm thinking, could we use another public works project like that. What do you think, Bob?"

"Roberto Cortez, Interior Secretary, thinks for a moment and then answers, "Maintenance of the national infrastructure always need workers and funds, and we are used to our budgets being flexible. The government adapts to deal with the unexpected disasters; so, it depends on what you are talking about."

"Well, Bob, I don't know about the funding, but the manpower pool will consist of every able-bodied eighteen-year-old young man and young woman in the United States."

Secretary Cortez is wide-eyed and open mouthed for a moment, then he asks, "What?"

"That's right; every eighteen-year-old. My primary goal is to restore patriotism in our young Americans.

"From what I experienced and heard from others, a hitch in the Military is cathartic for almost all young people; is that true Sheila?"

Colonel Sheila Murphy is representing General Porter who is still overseas in the China Sea.

"Yes," she replies, "When you live together, work together, eat together, play together; skin color, gender, language, where you were born and so forth lose their impact. Especially with combat troops. In combat all you care about is that soldier next to you; will he or she save my life; and will I save his or hers?"

The President looks at Secretary Cortez and says, "And that is all there is to that, Bob.

"I propose to give every young man and woman a two year internship on being a responsible, patriotic citizen.

"The young men and women will spend a one year in Military Service at an active Military base, fort or port, and then another year away from home at various construction sites, hospitals, schools, factories, farms and so forth.

The goal is for each conscript to meet a diversity of people from various regions of the country; to expose them to the variety and complexity our nation. So, they may be moved around a bit.

"Friendships will develop; tolerance and understanding will grow; pride in our diversity will re-appear.

"Generations of citizens will be created who are aware of a world of friends out there who share their hopes, values and pride in who we are, and what we do.

"That is Patriotism, and that can create miracles.

The President turns to the Secretary of Defense, Forest Sullivan and asks, "What do you think, Sully, can we afford this?"

"Oh, Hell yes. We can just postpone building the next aircraft carrier for a year or so, shelve a few of those experimental *'things'* we don't talk about. We can close a few foreign embassies, I think we just did that in China, didn't we? The point is wars are expensive. What you are proposing is pocket change."

"Thank you, Sully. Now we have manpower and funding.

"We have already developed a first draft of how this program would begin. You have a complete copy of the first draft in your mail.

"I will read from my copy. Colonel Murphy, please interrupt and correct me when I go astray.

She silently nods her head.

"It begins while the young citizens are still in school.

"During the first half of their Senior Year all students will have at least one class in Military Service and one class in Civil Service All the services will be described; their duties, requirements, responsibilities, geographic locations, salaries, career opportunities, et cetera.

"When practical, currently working recruitment representatives will visit the classes.

"During the second half of their senior year the students will visit and live on site for about two weeks, in the domiciles of the Services of their choice,

"At this point the duties and responsibilities of the young citizen will change. They are now young adults rather than students.

"Upon the graduation from Public School; the end of twelfth grade, the new young adults will receive notices of when and where to report for induction into the Military.

"The inductees will be sent to eight weeks of Basic Infantry Training.

"They will then be sent to various camps, forts, air bases, naval ports, et cetera. They will probably serve the remainder of their one-year commitment at this location.

"At the completion of their Military service, they will be given a two-week furlough.

"Those choosing a second year of Military will probably be ordered to a different location to maximize diversity of experiences.

"Those choosing a Civic Service will be given their furlough and orders of when and where to report to begin their second year of service.

"Many of the civil assignments will have barrack's style facilities; others will have living facilities similar to college dorms.

"Students sometime change their minds about their career choice; training schools do not have that kind of flexibility.   Petitions for changes of service choice will be accepted but it is discouraged.

"It complicates everything.

"Training schedules are prepared and set six months before classes begin. There is no viable way to honor such a request any quicker than six months, which lengthens the young adults time in service,

"The inductee is now a young adult; they made a decision; orders were cut and delivered. It is strongly suggested that the inductee suck it up, show up, try to be best inductee you can be.

"They are encouraged, or ordered to complete their commitment as chosen but each petition will be considered.

"At the completion of their one year of Military Service each citizen will receive his or her Notice of Completion of Military Service, and move on their year of Civil Service, or remain in the military.

"On completion of their second year they will receive a Notice of Completion of Military and Social Service. Society now regards them as Adult Citizens, entitled to all benefits and services of Citizenship.

"Many remain in the public employment and public housing for months or years as they pursue their civilian careers; but now they must pay rent, et cetera.

"The President pauses' stands up and says; "Let's take a stretch; there's more."

"The meeting members mill around for over ten minutes and then begin to return to their seats.

"When the President sits down the conversations stops.

"The President starts reading from his tablet, "Those with limiting disabilities will serve in positions they are capable of performing. A major purpose of this mandatory service is therapeutic; it is to give all citizens a sense of belonging in our society; and demonstrate that they are a valued member.

"Another goal is to bring to the attention of all citizens the value of our citizens with limitations. They are productive, they have most of the same capabilities, energy, emotions and needs as the rest of our citizens.

"And, they will be part of our countries work force; contributing to our economy.

"Women who have children or who are pregnant at age eighteen are still subject to the Public Service Obligation. If they chose not to fulfill their commitment at this time, they will be issued a High School Diploma without a Notice of Completion of Public Service.

"The Public Service obligation may be completed at some later date and the Notice will be issued.

"Men may also have personal or family reasons to postpone their Public Service. They also may petition for completion of their obligation through similar procedures if there is a good reason."

Interior Secretary Cortez closes his folder looks at President Heimdall "It looks like you are creating a military state."

"Somewhat," Heimdall replies, "But I'm not creating it, I am modeling it on real cultures form the past which were very successful, very efficient and productive.

"Medieval Germany was not a nation; it was a group of independent principalities held together by a common language. In the 1800's the principalities adopted mandatory, universal education and military training for all male children. By the late 1800's Germany was united as a nation where literacy was near 90%, all men knew the rudiments of military activities, and strong patriotism was a major character of the population.

"Near the same time Switzerland adopted a similar goal of education and took it one step further. Every male sixteen years old and above was in the Army Reserve. They were issued a rifle and ammunition which they kept in their home.

"The Reserves met once a year for a week or so to renew their military skills. At the end of training there was a marksmanship contest. The citizen soldiers were awarded medals and ribbons, which were highly prized.

"The awards were considered exhibits of a man's virility, bravery, reliability and responsibility. Men who did not participate in the contest were doomed to be childless bachelors the rest of their lives.

"For a more modern model of success I refer you to the Administration of President Franklin Roosevelt.

"He brought America out of the Great Depression of the 1930's with a great number of programs; the most notable were the work projects.

"He put the nations unemployed back to work on the nation's infrastructure. Everyone has heard of Boulder Dam; that was financed by the government, and employed thousands. When finished it supplied electric power, water, and recreation to that southwest corner of the country.

"But the government built other dams, power plants, highways, bridges, levees; it created parks and national monuments, and it goes on and on.

"Conservatives, reactionaries, and the ultra-rich ranted and raved but Roosevelt carried on and put the working class back to work, sent their children to school, instilled pride in all the social classes about what they could accomplish, and what the nation could accomplish.

"By the time Fascism appeared in Europe and Japan and their leaders decided to take on the United States of America our country had a trained and dynamic work force which could out produce the rest of the world combined.

"By the end of the end of the second year of that World War Two the American manufacturing machine, which was in production twenty-four hours a day, every day of the week, was turning out one cargo ship every four days, and one war plane every seven minutes; day and night.

"And our agriculture was feeding the world; if they were an ally. After the war, America was feeding the world while those countries devastated by that war recovered.

"Our country and our people were proud and honored to do it.

"It also made us the richest nation in the world

"Regaining that proud stature is a major goal of this admiration. These two years of universal social service, will introduce our eighteen and nineteen-year old men and women to each other, and to what our nation is all about.

"They will experience the diversity, the energy and power of our people, our culture."

The room is quiet for a full minute; then Roberto Cortez says, "That is a great speech, Mister President; but I'm already on board. You are going to need all that energy and power to accomplish *that* dream; there will be strong resistance from groups throughout the country."

"That is the reason it is to be Universal, there will be no loop holes or protective caves.

"Naturally, there will be some who really cannot serve. We cannot deal with those who need constant medical or nursing care; there is no point in drafting those who absolutely cannot read and write; those who cannot be trusted with anything with a sharp point, those who constantly have conversations with inviable friends.

"But, one of our goals is to create a sense of inclusion for those not meeting the standards for military service. They may perform quite well in other services."

"And, by the way, Bob; you and I are not the only ones in this room who have first names; when those doors are closed, first names are appropriate; unless I'm chewing your ass out.

"I know I'm the President; I know that you know I'm the President; so, if you don't mind ... ..."

"Understood. Woody, do you prefer Woodrow, or just Hey You?"

The President shrugged and answered, "Whatever."

"Well, Woody, this 'Universal commitment won't impact the Military much; combat troops will remain combat ready.

"Other units might have to build wheel chair ramps, special bath and toilet facilities, et cetera; they can; and will.

"But the other services might have to cope with more diverse populations with more limiting conditions. We don't have established protocols for this."

"I've thought some on that subject, and asked questions here and there. The military accepts requests for specific occupation assignments and they accept the requests, if they can.

"They consider the education and work experience of the recruit and try to match up assignments with abilities when they can. The rest are sent to training for combat skills. This happens while the recruit is in Basic Training.

"If this works for the Military, something like that should work for the other services."

"Do the other services have a something like Basic Training?"

"I don't think so; maybe they should."

After a few moments Secretary Cortez says, "I think they should; it wouldn't be that hard. The organization template should be the same for all departments.

"Day one: moving in, getting supplies and tools, and settling down.

"Day two: learning about the department what it does and who is what.

"Day three: individual counseling and assignment.

"Day four: let's get to work.

"I like it Bob, elaborate on the events of each day, write it up and get back to my desk as soon as possible.

The President looks around the table and asks, "Well?

"What else have you been thinking about? Speak up."

There were no volunteers.

The President continues looking around and catches the slight smile on Colonel Sheila Murphy's face.

He asks, "Maybe the Military has something thing to offer?"

The Colonel's smile disappears and she answers, "Mister President; I do have a few observations, Sir."

The President hesitates before he answers. "I would like hear them. And you can be 'at ease' when you talk to me. I just approved that ... and I am the President."

"Sir, I an Officer in the United States Army, on duty, in uniform, addressing the President of the United States.

"Sir, the Protocols are clear, concise and understood. May I continue with my assignment, Sir?"

After a long moment the President responds, "Please proceed, Colonel. "

"May I have a cleared room, Sir?"

"<u>Cleared room! ...</u> Wha... Why?"

"There is a good reason, it will become evident, Sir."

"He turns to his Chief of Staff and loudly says, "Lorraine, clear the room; take them on a half hour coffee break; tell the men on the door to check on me in ten minutes to make sure I haven't been assassinated."

When the Cabinet members returned a half hour later the President was alone in the room, the Colonel is gone.

Secretary Cortez nods his head towards the empty chair and raises his eyebrows.

Heimdall leans, toward Cortez and quietly says "I was getting to close to top secret stuff; she had to shut me up."

Cortez's brow knitted into a hard frown.

"She was right ... did the right thing ... she, sending an alternate."

Cortez shrugs, straightens up in his chair, and comments, "I believe we were about to discuss those who would choose to avoid service because they 'lust don't want to do it. Now that sounds interesting."

"We were; the President replies, "They will be given one reminder of their obligation and ordered to contact their Selective Service Board within fourteen days.

"Failure to comply is a violation of Federal Law; a warrant for their arrest will be issued and delivered to the Federal Marshall's Department. They will be arrested and held in Fort Leavenworth, Kansas until their trial can be scheduled."

"Wow, you are a hard ass, Mister President."

"Wait until hear about what I propose for the next group."

"Which group is that?"

"Those whose parents try to buy their child's way out of service."

The President smiles and says, "The same routine will be followed; two weeks' notice: then a warrant and arrest, if necessary, except the parents or guardians, and possibly others will be included. They will all be charged with aiding and abetting a felony.

"The child will be sent to Leavenworth; the parents will be held in local jails or prisons. Of course, most will be granted release by posting bond. But still under arrest and awaiting trial."

"How's that for hard ass, Bob?"

Still smiling the President shakes his head and asks, "Where did you grow up Bob?"

Bob replies "East Los Angeles, man;". "In a neighborhood called 'Presidio,'. Tough as any place in New York or Chicago or Houston."

"Oh, then I might guess your parents were not part of the financially secure class."

"That's right, Woody; I wasn't educated at USC, Stanford or any other of those elite schools.

"My education was gained from the alleys, playgrounds and streets of Presidio, and the 'prison camps' called 'public schools.'

I went to Los Angeles City College, for a while, did some correspondence schools, and my Bachelor's Degree is from an online college.

"I already had a PhD in life, survival, and politics from the streets of L.A."

"Impressive, Bob. For the time being I'm going to rely on you for what the working class is doing, saying and thinking. Okay?"

"I'm cool with that. Should I get myself a gun?"

"Hell, no! You couldn't get it past all those guards around this place."

"Wanta bet?"

The President thinks for a moment and then quietly replies, "Nope."

Vice President Steven Hightower and Attorney General Lawrence Nevins are quietly talking in the hallway. Nevins says, "Steve, I keep waiting and waiting, but nothing happens.

"We have to have a court system up and running or the rest of the government becomes autocratic.

"I have talked to Lorrain several times; she says it is on his calendar but more important matter keeps occurring."

"Larry, I know that and I agree, but he is really burdened with the China problem. We must see that China continues to move toward a truly democratic republic; and not return to communism.

"Yes, but we need to take care of our own government first.   First, Steve, not 'when we get around to it.'   The longer Woody governs by the edicts of one person the more difficult it will be to establish a democracy governed by the people.

"Woody has done a magnificent job getting rid of stagnant rotting government that preceded us, but he has done almost nothing to give us the new, streamlined and efficient Twenty-first Century Democracy we had hoped for.

"He has become obsessed with the 'China Problem,' and his drams of a utopian society modeled on his ideas."

Both men were quiet and thoughtful for few minutes. Then the Vice-President asks, "How do we get to him?   If he won't listed Lorraine who would he listen to?"

"I'll bet he would listen to General Porter."

"Probably, but he is in the China Sea conquering China."

"Hmm what about that officer, the one sitting in our meetings for General Porter

"You mean the woman who shut down our meeting so she could talk to Woody in private.

"I wonder what they talked about.

The Vice President comments, "Woody filled me in on some of that. It had to do with protocols and how to conduct meetings.

"She told him that the Cabinet members were not participating because they were confused. She told him using first names in meetings destroys protocols. Dump the first names; restore protocol."

"Wow."

"Yeah, she gave him a spanking. Then she recused herself because she had broken protocol."

The Attorney General asks, "Are you thinking what I am thinking?"

"I'll get my office on it. I'll follow up and get back to you.

"You have work to do; I'm just the Vice-President."

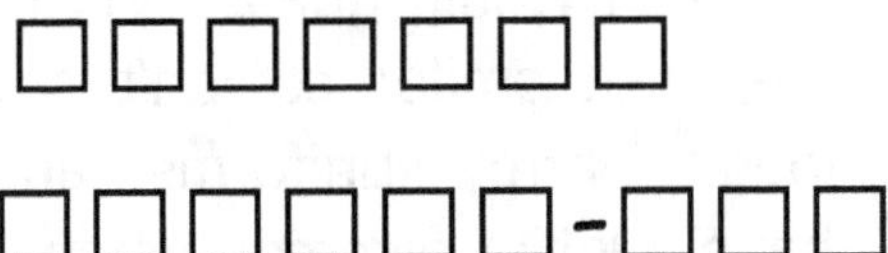

Celeste gives Woody a big hug; they are in the West Wing Office. Woody holds her tight for a little while and then asks, where are the children/'

"They went around back with one of the guards; they wanted to see their dogs."

"Oh, so seeing their Dad is less important than playing with their dogs?"

"Of course; you don't wag your tail or lick their faces.

"By the way, while we are on the tail wagging subject; I hear you have a new military advisor, some female Army Officer. Is there anything I should know?"

It was long moment before the President answers; "Her rank and name are Colonel Sheila Murphy. With General Porter involved in the China War the Pentagon selected her to function as the Pentagon's representative to the Presidential Staff meetings."

"Is she pretty?"

Woody thinks for a moment and then says "She's youngish, I would guess forty or so. Pleasant face, nice smile; couldn't say much else though; army uniforms and Islamic burkas have a lot in common when it comes to style and glamour."

Celeste chuckles and asks, "How much time did you spend trying to guess what her figure looks like?"

"Not much, she was lecturing me on protocol of meetings and how to fix what I messed up.

"Uh huh; giving you lessons."

"Come on, Cele; You've made your point. I want to hear about your meetings in Europe; but first I'm going out back and see our kids. I missed them."

Stanley Moore Heimdall, Lisa Moore Heimdall and two Jack Russell Terriers came rushing around a hedgerow near the back of the large grassy area. Stan races on by his father, Lisa jumps and is caught by Woody; the terriers are circling the group in some sort of esoteric terrier ballet.

Lisa give Woody a kiss on the cheek and says, "I love you, Daddy."

"I love you two, sweetheart."

Stanley walks over extends his hand and says," Bonjour, Papa."

His father replies, "Parles vous Francais, Stanley?"

'Aw, no, Dad. I'm not sure the French people can Parles vous. I'm going to stick with my Spanish.

"How did you and Mom ever learn all those languages you speak?"

"It is your Mother who is the linguist of the family; I just stick with English and Spanish.

"Your Mother can go almost anywhere on Earth and gossip with the women."

"I heard that."

Celeste is walking across the lawn from a door on the back portico of the White House.

Woody puts Lisa down and she runs over and grabs one or the terriers.

Celeste moves to Woody's side and puts her arm around his rib cage. Looking at the children and their dogs she states, "Beautiful, aren't they?"

"Yes, they are. "

They watch the cavorting on the lawn for a minute, then Celest quietly says, "I invited your Colonel Murphy over for tea later this week."

After a short pause Woody says, "Good, did you check my calendar?"

"No, you are not invited.

"Ah, just as well."

It was a short moment before she added, "You are part of the subjects we will 'gossip' about.

"I asked her to wear a casual civilian outfit; I want to show her around the garden.

"And I will give you my assessment of her figure."

Monty took a deep breath and sighed, "Okay, I'm looking forward to that"

Woodrow, **Frank Deming** and other friends reopen The New York Stock Exchange; other markets sone followed, then National Banks and Treasuries and the worlds largest economies were open for business; except for Russia, and its allies; and China.

Russia refuses to participate and China has no economy to open, as yet.

The China Administration Counsel plans on each region of China joining as they become stabilized.

Each Chinese nation must have a Central Bank and an independent Monetary Agency to monitor the Central Banks transactions. This agency will publish quarterly reports showing the financial status each nation's Central Bank.

These quarterly reports will include the amounts of the nation's gross national product and its national debt.

The Agency will calculate the allowable rate of leveraged debt and incorporate the figures into each nations budget. This will a quarterly based on each nation gross national product the preceding quarterly operation.

The Agency will have the authority to seize the control of the banks operations if they do not conform to the Agencies calculated and published rate of allowable leveraged debt for two or more consecutive quarters.

As soon as possible the governments will establish controls on transactions by Insurance Companies, commercial banks and stock market companies.

All these controls must be in place and operating within one year of the initiation of the documentation and enaction by the government of the nation.

China makes its debut as a nation with a capitalist economy

"Woody, practically every state in the Union is clamoring for elections."

The African-American man standing in the President's Office is the Superintendent of Penal Systems for the State of Illinois.

"There is no organized court system, nor have we shown that we are going to produce one. Kangaroo courts are springing up everywhere. There have been posse' executions but we have no data.

"Prisons are full to overflowing and the inmate facilities are beginning to look like something out of World War Two Nazi Germany.

"Food and clean water are becoming scarce.

"Some are beginning to let non-violent offenders just walk away and wander into nearby towns, or cities.

"Something has to be done right away. This is not what we promised the public; it is the exact opposite.

"If we don't turn our attention to the Legal and Justice, right now; there will be no tomorrow.

"Denzel, I thought the Governor of your state had things under control; he hasn't petitioned for any assistance. No one else from Illinois has complained, at least not directly to me."

"I have some pictures, the Superintendent says.

A darkness grows in the Presidents eyes as he growls, "Show me."

Denzel produces his smart-phone and hands it to the President.

For about ten minutes the President thumbs through pictures asking one- or two-word questions; receiving one- or two-word answers.

The President closes the smart-phone hands it back to Denzel and asks, "Have you made a copy of this for me?"

Silently Denzel produces a flash drive and hands it to the President.

While the President opens the safe in the bottom of his desk he asks, "what has the Governor been doing for the past six months?"

"I'm not sure Woody, but I am sure he was making money. You know; stealing, embezzling, selling appointments and contracts, et cetera."

The President closes the safe door and looks at the chair by the hall door where his Clerk, Chris Donovan usually sits, but Chris was already standing by his desk with his smart tablet out and ready.

"Chris, this is temporary top-secret communication. Get that Colonel Sheila Murphy at the Pentagon on my encoded line. Tell her it is a top-secret emergency. Then go get Lorraine and both you and Lorraine come back."

The President looks at Denzel and asks, "What did that governor do before he was Governor?

"Land developer, I think, shopping malls."

"Real Estate; ironic."

"How so?"

"He used to develop shopping malls and his next home will be a twelve foot by eight-foot cell."

Lorrain and Chris come into the office. Chris quietly closes the door goes back to his chair and watches the President

Lorraine asks, "What's up boss?"

"Well, Lorrain, as soon as I get in touch with the Pentagon, I'm going to send about a division of infantry to Springfield, the capital of the State of Illinois.

"They are going to seize and occupy the capital and arrest every elected official in the government. The charge is 'suspicion of treason.

"Each one will be held until NSA investigates their financials and either clears them, or charges them.

"Is that going to be a problem?"

After she quit laughing Lorrain says, "Well, first, do you have evidence of a crime."

"I do in my desk safe."

"Good, any witnesses?"

"Yes; May I introduce Denzel Brown, Supervisor of Incarceration Facilities for the State of Illinois."

Mister Brown nods.

Lorraine continues, "Mister Brown, are you willing to testify in a Court of Law to the veracity of the evidence you saw and photographed"

"Yes, I will."

The President looks at his Clerk and starts to say something, but stops, Chris is already beside his desk.

Chris closes his phone as he says, "A document processor with security clearance is on the way."

Loraine comments; "I hope she brings some extra forms with her; this might get complex."

Sousa march music is coming out of the President's desk. He retrieves his encoded phone, grins and says, "Pardon my sense of humor."

He says into the phone; "Good day Colonel Murphy; I need a small army for a while, I was wondering if you might just have one hanging around, doing nothing.

"Oh, but first, I have visitors with in my office, I'll relocate to the shielded room and call you back."

As he leaves the room he says, "Lorraine, start the Presidential Orders; it's all coming together."

When the President returns, he announces, "We are in luck. There is an infantry Brigade bivouacked at a camp about an hour's drive away from Springfield. That's about two hundred fifty men.

"They can be assembled and be in Springfield in about two hours. Intelligence should have the location of the buildings to be occupied by then.

"Colonel Murphy said she would establish contact with the National Security Agency and coordinate the occupation with them.

Turning to Denzel Brown the President asks, "How would you like to be a Governor pro-tem for a while?"

"Well, I ... for how ... who ... "

"Yes or no, Denzel."

"Ah, Yes."

"Good ... and thank you, we'll do the oath in a few minutes."

Looking across the room the President calls out, "Lorraine."

She quick steps over, extends two orders and says, "Sign these."

"What are they?"

"I'll explain later; or dome time, some day. Sign them!"

"I need the rest of the staff on deck."

"I have notified all of the Secretaries of the emergency meeting; they should all be here within a couple of hours.

"General Porter says he will join us by satellite."

"What the Hell, don't I get to do anything around here?"

"You already did; you hired good people. Now your orders about the Superior Court Systems ..."

"Let's swear in Denzel, first; I need him in Illinois as soon as possible."

Chris, who is standing a few steps away interjects "The helicopter has just arrived and an air cab at the airport is being fueled up."

The President glanced back and forth between his clerk and his Chief of Staff.

Lorraine taps the stack of papers on his desk and says, "The Superior Court System, Woody."

□ □ □ □ □ □ □

□ □ □ □ □ □ - □ □ □ □

Presidential Order # 126
Attn: all State Governors

All Superior and lower courts will open as soon as possible. Governors may contact the United States Treasury Department and apply for emergency funding for the cost of the courts.
Applications for Emergency Funding must be submitting within seven days of the receipt of this Presidential Order

Presidential Order # 127

Attn: all State Governors

 All State, County and City Police Departments will open as soon as possible. Governors may contact the United States Treasury Department and apply for emergency funding for the cost of the police departments.

All applications for Emergency Funding must be submitting within seven days of the receipt of these Presidential Orders.

All Courts and Police Departments must be operational within fourteen days of these Presidential Orders.

Failure to meet these deadlines will be considered acts of incompetence or insurrection by the non-complying Sate Governor. Said Governor's terms of office will end and they may face civil or criminal prosecution.

An interim Governor will be appointed by the office of the President.

"Impressive, I hope it works." Attorney General Lawrence Nevins is watching President Heimdall's face, hoping to get a hint of what is coming next.

The steely resolve in the Presidents eyes doesn't change.

He hands the order to his Chief of Staff, Lorraine Dumont. and says, "Send it."

She takes the order and leaves the room without uttering a word.

Lawrence Nevins asks, "Have you done anything about food, water and medical care for the prisons yet?

"I think so. We couldn't go to the National Guard without alarming the Governor's offices. So, I went to the Army. They have reserves of food and water all over the nation; and they have field hospitals with doctors.

"My contact says she will have logistics in place and supplies waiting to deliver to the prisons when we notify her that the arrests of the governors begin."

"That woman Colonel?"

"Yeah; that woman Colonel is the Commander in Chief of the Army until General Porter gets back from China."

"How many Governors do you expect to replace?"

"I don't know Larry; I don't know how deep the corruption and abuse of power got.

"Damn it! I went deaf, dumb and blind with our success with the China situation.

"I didn't get blind-sided, I got drunk on the champaign of success, stopped doing my job. I'm no better than those I'm prosecuting, just a damn fool with too much power.

"You're being a bit too harsh on yourself, Woody; we let you down. You would think at least one of your staff would have noticed something."

"Yeah, you were all playing follow the leader. But the leader has to know his priorities, seek out the minor cuts and scratches before they become infected and poison the whole damn body.

"Woody, you know Celeste is back, don't you?"

"Uh, yes; why do you ask?"

"Oh, I've known you both for a long time, and I've noticed that you both are better when you are together."

His neck tendons are tight and his face reddens as he turns and says, "So what are you suggesting, Larry; that all I need is to go play and little 'jump and hump' with my wife and these problems will solve themselves.

Larry grins, "No, Woody, some problems, but not these. I was referring to 'pillow talk.'   How long do you think Cele will put up with this pool of self-pity you are swimming in.

"Think about what she will say."

It was several minutes before the President calmly says, "Thanks, Larry, I do miss her, you know."

"Yes, we all do, she is the one of the brightest stars in our heaven."

"Indeed. Well, we have one Hell of a mess to fix and don't even have a starting point yet."

"Woody, may I suggest that the first problem, which will hit us tomorrow morning is "replacement Governors.'

"We can't use anyone in any of the current State administrations.

"I agree Larry, we need people with leadership abilities and who are comfortable being in the spotlight."

"If the FBI clears them, we could consider business and industrial executives.

"Even some sports coaches … or athletes … or entertainers."

Woody, this is getting confusing.

Suddenly, the Presidents face lights up, "we will run 'help wanted' ads Nationally.

"Apply by e-mail only, we don't have time for paper applications.

"And they don't have to live in the state they would govern, the positions are temporary, Federal appointments.

"Well, let's get started.   I think Lorraine would know something about how to go about this."

"She'll love it

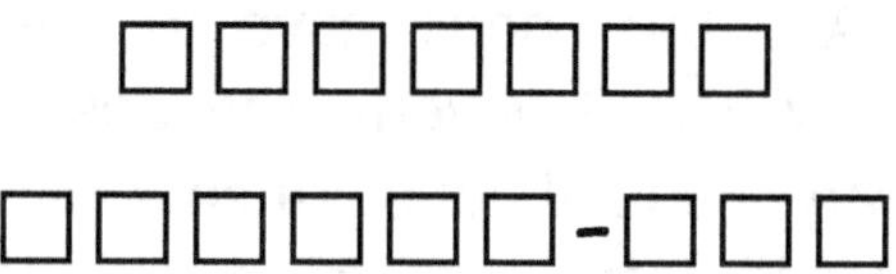

"Nice to see you again stranger, we were hoping you would drop by one of these days."

"I'm sorry Cele, we've almost reached a point where I can get back here on a regular basis."

"It's okay, Woody. I put a photo of you in each of the children's rooms so they will recognize you when you do come to see us.

"You do have sleeping quarters in the West Wing, don't you?"

"I have a fold up bed in one of the meeting rooms; I could sleep in the safe room in the basement but I get claustrophobic down there.

"It is so sound proof in there that when I wake up I don't know where I am, or if I'm alive, or if anything exists … anywhere."

"Why don't you put a television set down there?"

"That won't do it, I just want to keep me out there. Someone did put a radio down there that plays uninterrupted, soft music; like in elevators."

"Yuck; go upstairs a see our children; they are still up."

Woody the father came down after a half hour and became Woodrow the husband. He settles on the couch beside his wife and asks, "Well, what have you been doing for entertainment?"

"Who has time for entertainment. My secretary keeps me booked up for most of the day. Public relations mostly.

"I have all my meals with Stanley and Lisa. If or when you are on television, we watch you; but the children pay very attention to what is going on beyond their small world."

"Good for them, wish I could."

Cele smiles and continues, "Someday Woody; someday I'm just going to have you kidnapped and brought back home to play."

"Cele, what we are working on will dramatically change our lives."

"When?"

"A month or so, maybe."

"I hope so. You used to find a way to sneak out for a conjugal visit now and then; but it has been months; months, Woody!

"That was the reason I was acting so silly about Sheila."

"Sheila?"

"Oh; pardon me; Colonel Sheila Murphy.

"I'm not so good with protocols myself.

"When I heard about you and Sheila working together in private, one on one meetings, well my imagination went ballistic.

"After talking with her for a while I realized that she was not some sort of predator looking for some raw meat, or naïve twit looking for fame, fortune, and a book she could sell."

Woody is concentrating on what Celeste was saying, and has a slight smile on his face.

Celest continues, "We discussed limits, expectations, and protocol.

"Sheila admits she is a single woman in her late thirties who is 'married' to her career. She went to West Point right out of high school; she graduated near the top of her class.

"She was sent straight to Afghanistan, was in combat, demonstrated leadership, and quickly rose to the rank of Captain. Then she was sent all around the world and she became a Major, and then, well, I don't know where she went or what she did to come a Colonel.

"I guess you know all that, don't you?"

"Some of it, I didn't know she was in combat."

"I'm not surprised."

"Well, now, she is physically and psychologically fit, hale and hardy, and often horney. My guess is that you do not need to be briefed on that.

"She also stated that she noticed a 'normal' attraction to you; you are a 'hunk' you know. "But she says that it was well within accepted norms for our species."

"Our species! That's kind of a letdown. I'm now I'm just a species specimen!"

"Careful, Honey. If that bothers you too much, my imagination might take off again."

"Sorry; so, you and Colonel Murphy are friends now."

"We are friendly; she and I discussed the goals of our administration and the stress you have to absorb in your position.

"We are both dedicated to the success of the new government and will do whatever it takes to get the job done; whatever that may be.

"We decided we will continue to talk to each other about your reactions to the stress and what she could provide in my absence to assure your continued mental health."

"So, wherever I go, I will have someone to 'mother' me?"

"I've never known you to need mothering, Woody. "Think of her as a cousin, a kissing cousin, someone to talk with; ... and whatever."

United States of **Probably every television** in the Western Hemisphere is tuned to the State of the Union speech of President Woodrow Heimdall.

He is broadcasting from the President's Office in the West Wing of the White House. He is sitting at his desk.

"My fellow Americans, and citizens of the rest of the world, our Administration has decided that America is ready for democratic elections of a new Congress of the United States of America.

"We have come through some trying times. The closing and dissolution of our prior Congress; the revelations of the corruption and criminal activity of that Congress; and the despair of the American public due to what those criminals did to the vigor and happiness of our people.

"We have endured a brutal worldwide recession as a result of our investigation of the actions of these social and economic criminals.

"We, as a people, are still suffering each time more crimes are revealed as we continue investigations of the cesspools of corporate and personal greed and lust for political power.

"But we are recovering; we are Americans.

"The world is recovering, because Americans are world citizens.

"The World is also recovering, because that is what we human beings do.

"We never give up, we pick the pieces up, put them together, make something new where pieces are missing, often we create things that never existed before.

"We keep on working, we struggle, we sweat, we cry, we bind our wounds, we stand up and go to work; we won't, we can't, just lie down and die!

"Here at home, in America, the Constitution Committee has presented us with a series of changes that will reflect The Original Federal Constitution, the Bill of Rights, all other amendments to the Original Constitution, and all Supreme Court Decisions affecting the Constitution.

"The Committee also included a proposed age limit for Supreme Court Justices of ninety years.

"We have studied this new Constitution, debated each item, and made some minor changes to the document and decided to accept and enact the New Era Constitution as the replacement for the Original Constitution of the United States of America.

"As a companion piece to the New Era Constitution the Committee has presented us amendments and maps realigning and renaming the territory; land, sea, ice, and air, which is including within the national boundaries of what will now be known as the

"The Commonwealth of American Republics."

"The chart showing the new organization of the nation should be on your screens or monitors about now; copies will be available tomorrow or thereabouts."

Commonwealth of American Republics

North Pacific: "Evergreen Republic"
Three states: Washington, Oregon, Alaska.
Republic of California: "Golden State Republic"
Six states: Golden Gate, Sylvania, Central California, Big Valley, Mojave and Sierra, South California.
Great Plains Republic: "Big Sky Republic"

Nine states: Colorado, Utah, Idaho, Montana, North Dakota, South Dakota, Kansas, Nebraska and Iowa.

Southwest Republic: "Wild West"
Five States: Texas, Oklahoma, New Mexico, Arizona, and Nevada.

Great Lakes Republic: "Heartland"
Eight States: Minnesota, Wisconsin, Michigan, Illinois, Indiana, Ohio, Indiana, Kentucky and West Virginia.

New England Republic: "Patriots"
Six States: Maine, New Hampshire, Vermont, Massachusetts, Connecticut, and Rhodes Island.

Old Dominion Republic: "First Communes"
Seven States: Virginia, Maryland, Delaware, New York, Gotham (formally NYC), New Jersey and Pennsylvania.

Southeastern Republic: "Dixie"
Eight States: Arkansas, Tennessee, Louisiana, Mississippi, Alabama, Georgia, North Carolina, South

Carolina, (The Florida Panhandle and north central Florida is in the process of being annexed to Alabama and Georgia.

Territories and Protectorates
The District of Columbia
The Gulf Protectorate: Puerto Rico, South Florida, various other islands.
The Pacific Protectorate: Hawaii, Guam and other Pacific Islands.

The President continues, "This will be quite a change but once fully developed and implemented it will provide more and better service to the citizens, businesses, companies and institutions of our nation.

"We will now show charts of the Responsibilities, Powers and Funding sources of this new organization."

Federal   Responsibilities: Managing the Federal government, managing the Federal Military, international relations, international trade. Maintaining facilities for the Supreme Court system, parks and monuments. Immigration.

Federal Powers: Federal Marshalls, US Military, Secret Service, Executive Orders, National Security Agency, CIA

Federal Funding Source: Tariffs, federal portion of income tax

Republics Responsibilities: Collection and management of personal and corporate income tax. The national budget. The Treasury Department. Regulating interstate traffic and trade. Maintenance of interstate highway system.

Republics Powers: Federal Marshals, FBI, IRS, Census Bureau

Republics Funding Source: interstate traffic and shipping fees, business tax,

States Responsibilities: Regulation of business, manufacturing, agricultural, medical, social services, recreational facilities, et cetera. State Judicial System.

States Powers: State police, State business, manufacturing, and agriculture inspectors, medical and social service inspectors

States Funding Source: Sales tax

Districts (formerly Counties) Responsibilities: Utilities, roads, schools, , elections, libraries, public safety, lower courts, parks, parades, pubic events, district elections, etc.

Districts Powers;

Districts   Funding   Source:
Citizen approved bonds and taxes.

Judiciary: Federal, State; Criminal, Civil, Corporate, and special subject courts. Incarceration facilities.

"We know this is a lot to absorb at once, that this is lot of work, that there will be a lot of confusion, but the results will be great.

"So, let us begin!

"Tomorrow, I will issue Presidential Orders to commence with the reorganization.

"I hope the eternal spirit of tolerance, respect, and love will still be with us as we continue with our task."

After a long pause President Woodrow Heimdall sighs, looks at his cabinet members and continues, "I would like to announce at this time and place that I will not seek a second four-year term as

President of this country or any other elective office.

"When I ran for the position of President two and a half years ago, I promised to fix this dysfunctional circus our government had become. That was my only goal.

"Completing that goal will take a long time, and maintaining a functional government will be a never-ending task.

"That task must be undertaken by future generations, generations who see, understand and work within the awareness of eternal change.

"My administration has laid the foundation for a better society, but it will be the task of each new generation to continue to build a transparent, open and honest citadel of righteousness and honor.

"I have used the methods of an autocrat to achieve the goal of changing a sick society into a recovering society which can have a glorious future.

"There is an old saying, "That power corrupts and absolute power corrupts absolutely. "

"I believe that; and that is the reason I must be replaced with a democratically elected successor.

"I will finish out my four-year term by continuing to work for changing areas not yet modified or working well.

"I want to see government buildings, green areas … even parking lots, that are lobbyist free.

"That may be an impossible dream, but we might be able to fence in a 'government campus' and grant access to only those who work there or are temporarily there for specific reasons.

"We could create an inner city where employees and elected officials could go to the toilet without a lobbyist following them with rolls of toilet paper. It might be a productive system to try.

"And if I were King … oops, there goes that absolute power thing again.

"It must be time for me to shut up, sit down, and get back to work.

"I would like to leave you with one thought; 'We must always protect our Democracy, our Commonwealth of Republics legal system, and right of all citizens be free within those laws.

"That is about all I have to say. There is work to do; I had better get back to doing it, while I still can do it."

"I'm hearing good things about your trip; you are turning out to be quite an ambassador.

"It is fun Woody, I enjoy the travel; new places, new people. And this time I didn't have to worry about the children."

Woody and Celeste are strolling through the White House rose garden.

"How did you do with them: did they drive you crazy?"

"No, you know how that is. Lisa is a little charmer and has assumed the Secret Service is her private army. She leads her guards around the premises like she is a queen, but a kind a loving one.

"The guards love it."

Celeste smiles as she says, "We'll have to bring her back to reality soon or she will become impossible as a teen."

"That's almost a decade away."

"It will be on us in a flash, My Dear.

"So, how was Stanley?

"No trouble at all; he's discovered reading. Not e-books, but real, hard cover and paper page books. He has a cheap, cloth book bag he carries with him everywhere."

"That's good, isn't it?"

"I guess so, most of the time.

"Oh, did something go wrong?"

"Not exactly; I had to confiscate one book he had; it was a little beyond his age; a romantic novel; a very detailed romantic novel."

Celeste's laughter dances through the roses. She says, "He's growing up to be just like his father, a bookworm, an intellectual, *horney* bookworm."

Woody grins and replies, "And Lisa is growing up to be just like her mother. She has a parade of men following her around like puppy dogs, and loving it."

"That's good isn't it, she'll never be lonesome."

It was a moment before Woody answers, "Yes, it is. You know, you are a great ambassador and negotiator."

"I enjoy it, Monty, and I know what I'm doing. That makes it fun.

"I wish I could be with you more often, but you know, and I know we need freedom to be who we are."

"Yes, Cele, you and I both know that freedom is one of the things that keeps us a family, that, and our privacy.

Celest frowns and growls out, "God damn reporters I guess you saw the photo."

"Reporters come with the territory, Cele; it will die down after I'm no longer in office."

"I suppose, but you know what bothers me most is the lies. The truth might be embarrassing; and somewhat inconvenient, just human beings being human.

"But these reporters have to create all sorts of disgusting, sordid things that never happened.

"I know and agree Cele, but reporters have to make a living, and they had pictures."

"But that reporter treated Pierre like he was some sort of sexual predator."

"Is that his name, Pierre?"

"Yes, Pierre; Pierre Auraunt. He is the French Commissioner of Culture."

"The article said he was married."

"He and his wife separated years ago, they had a marriage agreement like ours and they didn't need a divorce. They do have children."

"Is something bothering you about Pierre?"

"Oh, no. I was just wondering; the photo surprises me."

"Pierre and I had dinner that evening, at that restaurant."

Woody and Celeste are silent as they continue their stroll through the rose garden.

Finally, Celeste says, "I do seem to recall now, that it was a little more than just dinner."

Woody smiles as they continue to walk, he quietly comments, "Thank you; Cele, we need to remember our agreement, 'open and honest"

"Well, you weren't exactly 'open and honest' about your romantic Colonel."

"I had to keep quiet about Sheila, she would be kicked out of the Army for having sex with the President!"

"You could have stopped that."

"Wouldn't that have made good headlines."

"Oh, let's forget about it. But tell Sheila to call me; while in Paris I picked up some of that lingerie she's been looking for.

"Or would you like me to wrap it for you so you could present to her yourself?

"Or would that be against some protocol or another?"

Woody looks at Celeste for a long moment; he then begins to laugh.

Then Celeste begins to laugh, too.

They are still chuckling and holding hands as they walk back toward the White House.

□□□□□□□

□□□□□-□□□

Ten years later.

The Heimdall family still lives in Montreal, Quebec Canada. They have a large estate.

Son Stanley, has a BA in International Economics from Ohio State Univ. He is currently enrolled in Harvard School of

International Law. Like is mother he is fluent in English, Spanish and several other languages.

Daughter, Lisa is enrolled in Beaux Arts Academie in Paris France. She is also multi-lingual.

Woody splits his time between his estate in Montreal, Canada; New York City and Washington D.C. He writes, occasionally is a guest speaker.

He sternly stays out of politics.

He still sees Colonel (now General) Murphy; and others, it is rumored.

Celeste splits her time between the estate in Montreal and other major world cities, especially Paris, France.

She is a roaming Ambassador at large for the Commonwealth of American Republics.

Her relationship continues with Pierre Auraunt.

□□□□□□□

□□□□□□-□□□□□

Commonwealth of American Republics

A couple of border wars were put down by Federal Marshalls. The Supreme Court ruled they could do that, it was their job.

National Military was for International disputes, and was not authorized to intervene in disputes between Republics.

Republic Guards could 'protect the Republic's interests within the borders but not transgress into adjacent Republics territory. This could result in the Federal Marshalls intervention.

It took a couple of years but the Superior courts and lower courts are functioning normally.

Police, Fire, and Emergency Medical services have returned to their traditional conditions; under paid and under staffed.

And most of the population is peaceful and happy.

Most of modifications initiated during the Heimdall presidency are functioning well.